# A Rather Unusual Romance

By

Stevie Turner

# A Rather Unusual Romance

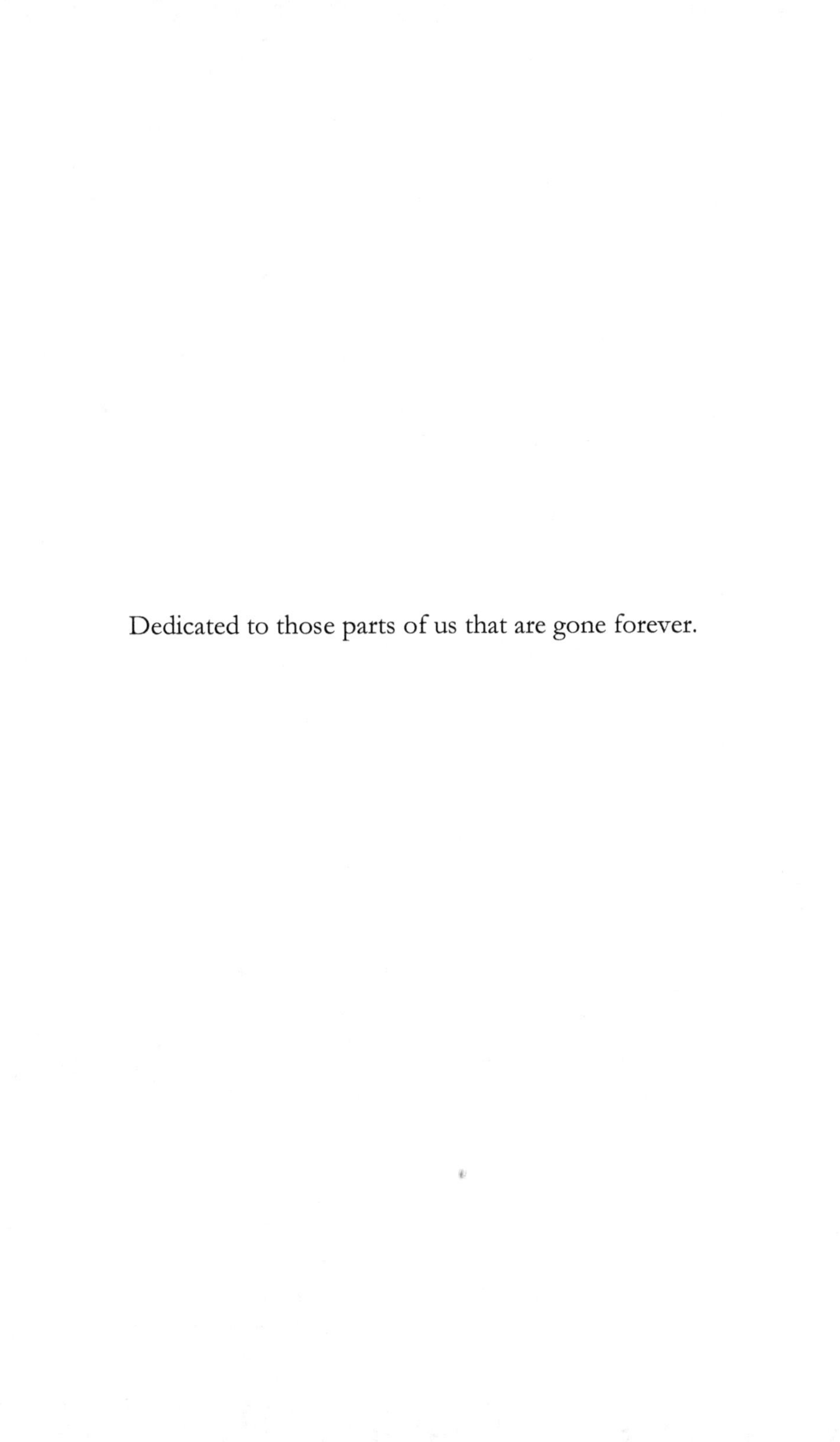

Dedicated to those parts of us that are gone forever.

# SYNOPSIS

Erin Mason, divorced and with two teenage sons, finds her world starts to fall apart when she undergoes what is termed a 'life event', and is diagnosed with cancer. Not too far away somebody else, Alan Beaumont, is also suffering a similar fate. Their paths slowly come together in this inspiring and sometimes humorous tale which shows how love can flourish in the most unlikely of circumstances.

# Table of Contents


CHAPTER 1 .................................................................... 1
CHAPTER 2 .................................................................... 7
CHAPTER 3 .................................................................... 13
CHAPTER 4 .................................................................... 19
CHAPTER 5 .................................................................... 27
CHAPTER 6 .................................................................... 31
CHAPTER 7 .................................................................... 37
CHAPTER 8 .................................................................... 41
CHAPTER 9 .................................................................... 45
CHAPTER 10 .................................................................. 49
CHAPTER 11 .................................................................. 53
CHAPTER 12 .................................................................. 57
CHAPTER 13 .................................................................. 63
CHAPTER 14 .................................................................. 67
CHAPTER 15 .................................................................. 73
CHAPTER 16 .................................................................. 79
CHAPTER 17 .................................................................. 83
CHAPTER 18 .................................................................. 89
CHAPTER 19 .................................................................. 95
CHAPTER 20 .................................................................. 101
CHAPTER 21 .................................................................. 107
CHAPTER 22 .................................................................. 111
CHAPTER 23 .................................................................. 117
CHAPTER 24 .................................................................. 121
CHAPTER 25 .................................................................. 125
CHAPTER 26 .................................................................. 129
CHAPTER 27 .................................................................. 133
CHAPTER 28 .................................................................. 137
CHAPTER 29 .................................................................. 141
CHAPTER 30 .................................................................. 147
CHAPTER 31 .................................................................. 151
CHAPTER 32 .................................................................. 157
CHAPTER 33 .................................................................. 161
CHAPTER 34 .................................................................. 165

CHAPTER 35.................................................................. 171
CHAPTER 36.................................................................. 177
CHAPTER 37.................................................................. 183
CHAPTER 38.................................................................. 189
CHAPTER 39.................................................................. 195
CHAPTER 40.................................................................. 199
CHAPTER 41.................................................................. 205
CHAPTER 42.................................................................. 211
CHAPTER 43.................................................................. 215
CHAPTER 44.................................................................. 219
CHAPTER 45.................................................................. 223
CHAPTER 46.................................................................. 229
CHAPTER 47.................................................................. 233
CHAPTER 48.................................................................. 239
CHAPTER 49.................................................................. 243
CHAPTER 50.................................................................. 247
CHAPTER 51.................................................................. 255
EPILOGUE ..................................................................... 259
OTHER BOOKS BY STEVIE TURNER......................... 263

# CHAPTER 1

"CAN YOU TELL me where I have to wait for the next train to New Cross please?"

The little old lady stood at the reception counter dishevelled and distressed. Erin Mason sighed, and stood up for the fifth time in as many minutes.

"Come on Rosie, I'll show you."

Taking hold of the gnarled fingers on Rosie's left hand, Erin slowly led the elderly woman back to her bed again.

"Here's where you wait." She cleared a few toast crumbs from the bedside armchair, and manoeuvred stiff and unyielding bones into a seated position. "The train will be along in a minute."

"What train? I don't want to get on a train."

"Well, just sit here in the waiting room then, and have a bit of a rest."

On her way out of bay 3 she let a silent expletive escape from her lips at the irritating sight of a junior doctor now sitting at *her* desk, using *her* computer, and blatantly ignoring the phone that was ringing incessantly. Erin spoke into the receiver as she stood menacingly over the doctor, who purposely ignored her presence.

"Somerset ward. Can I help you? This is the ward clerk."

"When's Walter's funeral?"

"Pardon?"

"Walter Tricker, poor old sod. Someone told me he'd snuffed it."

"Well, whoever told you was wrong. I can see him sitting up in bed. He's eating his breakfast at the moment." Erin reluctantly ceased burning a hole in the junior doctor's back, and shifted her gaze towards bay 4 for confirmation. Walter had finished his porridge and was washing it down noisily with great slurps of tea.

"You've made my day! Cheers, darlin'!" The phone went dead.

Erin sighed with annoyance at the caller's patronising tone, at the junior doctor, and at life in general.

*I'm not your darling!*

Almost at once the shrill ringing recommenced. Erin hoped against hope that it was not Mrs True's daughter. The junior doctor stood up and collected his patient's biopsy result from the printer, and Erin jumped back into *her* chair, *tutting* with annoyance at the sight of his enquiry which was still on *her* screen.

"Ward clerk. Can I help you?" She logged him out with a flourish.

"How is Edith True today?"

"Who's speaking please?" She recognised the cut glass accent straight away.

"It's her daughter."

The recent tell-tale death rattle emanating from the first bed on the left in bay 5 was quite audible. Poor Mrs True was not long for this world, but Erin knew it was not her job to inform the patient's daughter of the fact, and she was also under Staff Nurse Grey's strict instructions not to bother her while she was in handover. Instead of the usual glib reply of the patient having had a good night, she had to think of something else, and quick.

"No change."

"Tell her I can't get in to see her until tomorrow."

Erin was certain that Mrs True was past caring about whether her snotty daughter came in or not. However, a professional manner had to be adopted at all times.

"Yes, I'll tell her.  Thank you for calling."

"Darlin', 'elp me." Tommy Beale appeared from the side room and made his way towards Erin.

"Not this side of the desk, Mr Beale. You know that." Erin waved the elderly man away.

"Sorry darlin'. Can you 'elp me? Can you 'elp me, darlin'?" He shuffled to the front of the desk.

"Yes, I can help you. But before I do, let's get one thing straight. I'm not your darling.........okay?" She picked up a white board marker and rose to her feet.

There was a short pause while this information was digested. Finally Tommy nodded at Erin.

"I know that, darlin', but can you 'elp me?"

He had shuffled away before she could think of a suitable pithy reply.

As she updated the patient arrivals and discharges board for the day staff, she was aware that Staff Nurse Wright had popped her head around the side door and was hissing in her direction.

"Erin, can you call Mrs True's daughter please? We're putting her on the End of Life pathway now."

"She called a little while ago. She says she can't get in until tomorrow."

"Mrs True won't last that long."

"I just told her there was no change!" Erin's heart began to beat faster.

"Why did you tell her that? You should have spoken to Wendy first." Becky Wright whispered and came in closer.

"Wendy said not to bother her while she was handing over." Erin closed her eyes and tipped her head up to the ceiling. "Sorry." She exhaled a long sigh.

"That bloody woman!"

"I'll call her now." Erin put down the white board marker and moved towards the phone.

"Oh, and Erin…"

"What?"

"Don't be alarmed, but I think I just noticed something on the front of your neck when you were looking upwards."

"Eh?"

"It's my job to notice these things. I think you may have a little lump. Were you aware of it?"

Erin felt under her chin.

"I can't feel anything."

"Lower down where you have a little hollow." Becky pointed out the area on herself.

Erin tentatively pressed a finger into the base of her neck and relaxed with a smile.

"Oh, that; it's been there for years."

"Fair enough then. Let me know about Mrs True's daughter."

"Will do."

# CHAPTER 2

"MUM, KIERAN'S BEING a pain in the arse."

Erin took no notice as her 16 year old son Kevin, his short red hair unusually out of place, came into the kitchen staggering under the weight of his equally flame-haired twin brother, who was clamped to his back like a leech.

"Kieran, stop being a pain in the arse." Erin absentmindedly stirred a pan of hollandaise sauce with a wooden spoon.

"He can't help it, he was born that way." Kevin doubled over and fell to the floor.

"Boys; put a sock in it. Go and play on the motorway or something."

"That's nice; our own mother wants us to get run over." Kieran thumped his brother and kicked him on the shin. "That's for saying I'm a pain in the arse."

"Dinner's ready. Come and sit down for God's sake."

Erin was tired. She wanted to soak in a hot scented bath. She wanted the twins to shut up. She wanted an hour's peace and quiet. She flicked a stray strand of red hair behind her ear.

"Kevin, it's your turn to wash up tonight. Kieran can dry. I'm going to get in the bath after dinner. I'm knackered." She felt almost too exhausted to eat.

"Are you all right, Mum?" Kevin was instantly full of concern, causing Erin to smile at him.

"I'm just tired, that's all; had a busy day on the ward, and Mrs True died. I'd grown rather fond of her."

"You're too soft for that job."

"I know. I love it, but sometimes it just gets to you." She idly speared a sliver of salmon onto her fork. "How was college today?"

"Work experience next week. I'm going to be a plumber's mate. I'll get all the crap jobs, I expect."

"There's a joke there somewhere." Kieran poured more sauce onto his salmon steak. "I'll be in the bakery at the supermarket, with all the cakes I can filch."

"Hope you throw up." Kevin helped himself to more new potatoes.

"At least I won't have my hand up someone's u-bend."

"You'll need some bus money to get home then." Erin hoped there would be enough money left in her purse by then.

"Cheers, Mum. I'm skint." Kieran took the last of the new potatoes in the pot.

"It's okay. I've got some money saved from my paper round." Kevin gave his twin a supercilious look.

"Turd-boy." Kieran located his brother's leg under the table and gave it a kick.

"Shirt-lifter."

Usually she joined in with the boys' banter, but that night Erin had had enough.

"I'm going to get in the bath now, and have my dinner later. I'll leave the pair of you to clear up." She stood up to put a microwave plate over her dinner and put it to one side. "Is it youth club tonight?"

"Yeah, but I'm not going; it's boring." Kevin put down his knife and fork and stretched.

"Only 'cos Zoe's stopped going." Kieran winked and grinned.

"It'll leave the field clear for you and Denise."

"Just as long as I'm at one end of the field and she's at the other end."

"That's not what you said last week."

Leaving her sons tucking into a plate of home-made apple crumble, Erin went upstairs, locked the bathroom door, and sat on the edge of the bath with her eyes closed, drinking in the peace and quiet for a few moments. Remembering the bath plug had come loose from the chain again, she opened her eyes and stood up to search for it, finding it at last under Kieran's flannel. Turning on the taps, she added some scented foam and let the bath fill up whilst she divested herself of her clothes. She stepped into the welcome hot water, sank down into the bubbles, and relaxed.

As she lay there soaking, she thought back to Becky Wright's comments earlier in the day. Rinsing the soap off her right hand she felt the area at the front of her neck again. The little swelling was still there, just as it had been for some time. *The swelling……the lump!* She sat up in the bath with the sudden grim realisation that if it was visible to Becky, then perhaps it could have grown bigger? *She had a lump! Why on earth hadn't she done something about it before now?*

The long relaxing soak was spoiled. She hurriedly washed, and with a towel around her rushed into her bedroom and closed the door. She could hear the boys downstairs still clearing up after dinner as she picked up the extension and dialled the number she knew by heart.

"Good evening; Goldmark Surgery. Can I help you?"

Erin thought the receptionist sounded as smug as smug could be, in the safe knowledge that she was healthier than everybody else around her.

"Can I make an appointment with the doctor please?" "There's nothing now until Thursday." "This is urgent."

"What's the trouble?"

"That's what I want to tell the doctor." She hated doctors' receptionists with a passion.

"Come along to the surgery this evening at seven then, although you might have a long wait. I'll put you on the end of Doctor Draper's list. Can I have your name please?"

"Erin Mason. 24 St. Faith's Close, Goldmark Estate."

"I'll add you on at the end." "Thank you."

*Bitch!* She would just have enough time to take Kieran to his youth club.

There were still a few coughing and sneezing patients sitting patiently waiting by the time she arrived at the doctor's surgery. Erin tried to sit as far away from them as possible, and sighed with relief when her name appeared on the digital call board.

"Hello doctor." She smiled at the elderly lady sitting at her desk near the door.

"Hello Mrs.......er."

"Ms"

"Ms Mason. What can I do for you?"

Dr Draper swivelled her chair around.

"I've got a lump in my neck." Erin pointed out the area with a forefinger.

"How long has it been there?" The doctor peered intently.

"About six months at least, I think."

"Can you swallow for me please?"

Erin hated anybody touching her neck; even Chris had known not to go there. The doctor probed and prodded, as Erin swallowed and gulped to order.

"Hmm. I think you may have a little cyst on your thyroid. Do you know about your thyroid gland?" Doctor Draper stepped back and looked at her through thick rimless spectacles.

"Of course. It's to do with how quickly you burn up calories from food." *Did the doctor think she was stupid?*

"That's right. I'm going to refer you Dr Levine, an Endocrinologist at the hospital. He'll be able to check that your thyroid is working properly. Is that okay with you?"

"I suppose so." She sighed and wondered how long it would take for Stella, Dr Levine's secretary, to start the hospital grapevine buzzing.

"The wait shouldn't be too long; probably about two weeks."

At that point she wished she did not work at the hospital, because only a two week wait suddenly started alarm bells ringing in her head; some patients on the ward often complained bitterly to her they had waited three months to see a consultant.

*The GP considered her case was urgent!* Her heart started to race with the sure and certain knowledge of what that implied.

# CHAPTER 3

THE PENIS MADE a faint, almost imperceptible slapping noise as it fell on the desk in front of her. She had been trying to concentrate on filing continuation sheets correctly into a set of discharged patient's notes, but her recent visit to the GP surgery had started to prey on her mind. However, when she looked up, her train of thought was lost completely.

"George; where are your pyjamas?"    She suppressed a grin.

"Errr……..."    George Riley shook his head, with a hangdog expression on his face.

She signalled to Trixie, one of the health care assistants.

"Trix; we have a problem here!" "So I see!"


Erin tried to keep a straight face as she watched Trixie expertly grab a hospital gown from the clean linen trolley and pop it over George's head.

"I expect Mr Beale has had another of his little attacks." She whispered conspiratorially.

"Yes, I found three sets of pyjamas under his bed yesterday morning." Trixie smiled. "Come on George, let's go."

Erin watched George's departing back as he trailed a thin stream of urine behind him. Two familiar figures appeared in her peripheral vision and began to advance towards the desk.

"Can you 'elp me, darling?"

"Tommy, did you take George's pyjamas?" "'Elp me, 'elp me."

"Where do I wait for the next train to Bromley-by-Bow?" Rosie, naked except for a soiled incontinence pad on her head, stood patiently beside Tommy Beale.

"Trix; what's going on here this afternoon?" She shouted over the ringing phone, as a harassed Trixie came hurrying towards Rosie.

"We're short-staffed. There's just me and Sonia for three bays!"

Erin picked up the receiver.

"Somerset ward. Ward clerk speaking."

"Erin, it's Stella."

"Hi Stella." Erin knew exactly what was coming.

"Your GP has faxed through a referral. Dr Levine has a cancellation slot this afternoon. Can you come at 4.30?"

Erin imagined Dr Levine's secretary reading the referral letter as she spoke, and riffling through her notes with interest. Her heart sank at the thought of it. She absent-mindedly fingered the lump at the front of her neck.

"Yes, okay."

"Great. I'll let Appointments know."

The endocrinologist took a second glance as she walked into the consulting room.

"Hello. Haven't I seen you somewhere before?"

"I'm a ward clerk, Dr Levine. I work on Somerset ward. I'm always running around the hospital." Erin tried to hide the nervousness from her voice.

"Ah; of course! I have a letter from your GP here that says you've found a lump in your neck."

"Yes, he thinks it might be a little cyst on my thyroid." She had almost convinced herself of the fact.

"Well, we'll do some blood and urine tests to find out, and also an ultrasound scan and possibly a needle biopsy. How does that sound?"

"Is all this necessary?"

"As I'm sure you're fully aware, we have to rule out the small possibility of cancer. Is there any history of thyroid disease or thyroid cancer in your family?"

Erin thought long and hard. She could come up with no definite answer.

"Not that I know of."

"That's in your favour then for a start. How old are you now?" He checked the notes as he spoke.

"Forty two."

"You're still a young woman. I'm sure you'll be fine. Now, if you go along to Pathology tomorrow and collect some twenty four hour urine bottles, you can fill them up over the weekend and bring them back again on Monday and have your blood tests then. There'll be some instructions with the bottles. I'll send a request off for the ultrasound scan." He handed her a yellow ticket. "Present this at

Pathology when you collect the containers."

"Is that all?"

"I'll have a feel of your neck now, if that's okay with you?"

"Yes, it's fine."

She watched the doctor wash his hands, and then closed her eyes and thought of sunny beaches.

"Can you swallow for me, please?"

As his probing fingers dug right into the lump, Erin wanted to shout out but managed to tear her mind away at the last moment back to white sands, blue skies, and tall palm trees swaying in the tropical breeze.

"That's all for today. I'll see you again soon with all the results after you've had your ultrasound."

She came face to face with Kevin at the front door just as she was fishing for her key.

"You're late, Mum. Where have you been?"

"I had a doctor's appointment. Didn't you get my text?"

"Oh yeah, I forgot. Are you ill then?"

She smiled at the look of concern on her son's face. "I'm fine. Don't worry. The doctor thinks I have a cyst on my thyroid. He wants to check that it's okay, so I've got to have some tests. I've got to fill these up for a start." She held up the two 24-hour urine bottles.

"What have they got to do with your thyroid? Isn't that in your neck?" He looked perplexed.

"Don't ask me; I've just got to fill them up and go back for the results. Where's your brother?"

"He cycled over to Dad's place." "Why?"

"Freddie wanted some help with his science homework."

"Why didn't he ask Dad or Marie then?"

"Dad's working late and well, Marie is Marie isn't she? Freddie was going to swap some computer games with him afterwards, so that's probably the real reason he went, along with Marie giving him some dinner I expect. What's for *our* dinner? I'm starving."

"Can you nip down to the chippy? I don't fancy cooking tonight. Get whatever you want, and some plaice and chips for me please." She searched in her purse and handed over a ten pound note. "And bring back the change." Her two beady brown eyes shot him a knowing look.

"Can I get a gherkin as well?"

"Two; one for me please." She smiled at him and was rewarded with a hug.

# CHAPTER 4

ALAN BEAUMONT HATED his teeth. For years the bastard gnashers had been the bane of his life; they had been drilled, filled, bridged, x-rayed enough times to make him glow in the dark, and now in middle age two cracked molars with recurrent infections had been replaced by implants that had cost him a small fortune.

He looked at himself in the hall mirror, lifted his head and opened his mouth; *two new white veneers on the front crowns made him look like Ed, the Talking Horse, from that kiddy programme his daughter used to watch.* He sighed and carried on looking at himself; that lump at the base of his neck he had noticed a while back was not going away, and did not feel like part of his Adam's apple. He fingered the small swelling; it felt firm to the touch. He swallowed, and noticed how the lump moved up and down. *He would have to go and visit the Quack.........*

"Mirror, mirror on the wall, who is the fairest of them all?" Matilda Beaumont, fresh-faced, strawberry blonde, 18 years old and achingly beautiful like her mother, came downstairs and smiled.

"Well it ain't me for sure." Alan turned away from the mirror and suddenly wished he was twenty years younger.

"Yes it is; you'd make someone a lovely husband!" She put her arms around her father's middle and squeezed.

"I did once, but your mother never realised how lovely I actually was."

"All water under the bridge now; time to move on." Matilda ruffled his still-thick salt-and-pepper hair, and turned to take her sweatshirt off the coat hook.

"And I have; it's just that I'm too old now to go through all that again." He checked in the mirror surreptitiously once more to gauge the size of the lump.

"Nonsense; you're only fifty. You're hardly Methuselah." Matilda stared at him as she wriggled into the sweatshirt's sleeves. "What are you looking at in the mirror?" She came and stood back in front of him.

"Nothing." He jumped away. "Be careful driving; where are you off to tonight?"

"Just out with Matty; we're only going to the cinema. I won't be late." She kissed his cheek.

"I'll wait up for you."

"There's no need. I'm fine, honestly."

"Well, phone if you need anything."

"I will."

With a small stab of envy Alan watched his only daughter walk jauntily to her car, and drive off without a care in the world. Should he have bought her that car for her eighteenth birthday? Had he been too liberal a father? No, it was all good; at least she didn't have to face the lowlife on public transport at night, and he didn't have to listen to her complain about how he was turning into 'Uncle Buck' and ruining her social life. He ran a hand through his unruly mop of hair to smooth it down after its recent ruffling, and for the umpteenth time mentally pictured himself as he had been at the magic age of eighteen with his whole life before him, as though conjuring up the image might have somehow made it real.

*If he could live his life all over again, would he have married Tina for a second time?* Alan knew the answer to that one already; *if he was ever given another chance he would never be ruled by his loins again, and would pick somebody more homely-looking.* He chuckled however at the thought that had just entered his head; *unlike sensible fifty-somethings, weren't all eighteen year olds ruled by their loins?*

Nodding sagely to himself, he closed the front door, and then took another look at the lump in his neck in the mirror before searching in his address book for the phone number of the doctor's surgery.

"Good evening; Health Centre, can I help you?"

He tried to picture the owner of the pleasant female voice on the other end of the line, but assumed she would probably have been snapped up by some marauding male many years before, and would more than likely than not put the phone down in disgust if he dared to ask her out for a drink.

"Could I book a doctor's appointment please?"

"We have one tomorrow evening at seven o'clock with our locum."

"Yes please; Alan Beaumont, twelve Moffatt Court."

"That's all booked for you; we'll see you tomorrow then."

Without his daughter's company for the evening, Alan could already feel the pangs of loneliness waiting to envelop him. He wandered into the kitchen and switched on the kettle. Putting a spoonful of coffee into a mug, he loaded the dishwasher while waiting for the water to boil. Satisfied that two days' worth of dirty crockery was at last having a well-deserved wash, he took the steaming mug of coffee into the front room and pressed a button on the remote to switch on the TV:

"Fuck all on again." He mumbled to himself as he hopped through the channels. He sat back in the armchair with a sigh and tried to blot out the picture in his mind of Matthew Jardine, *his apprentice for fuck's sake!*, trying it on in the darkness of the cinema with his daughter; *his princess!* His hands involuntarily bunched into fists at the thought of it, before he laughed ruefully and relaxed. *What was the point of getting worked up? Tilly had probably been deflowered ages ago! She was eighteen, beautiful, savvy, and had always had a string of boys at her beck and call.*

*Well.........good for her.*

*Let her go; she's got to grow up. If she comes back, then she loves me. If she doesn't, then Tina must have finally won her over.*

Finding a suitable film at last, Alan settled down for the evening and lost himself in a war drama, absentmindedly noticing the time on his wristwatch when the closing credits eventually rolled by. *Ten past eleven; Tilly should have been home by now!*

He went to the window and peeped out under cover of the heavy curtains; his daughter was just parking her car. Jumping away guiltily, Alan turned out the lights in the front room, ran to the hallway, and flicked on the porch light.

"Hey, Dad. I hope you weren't waiting up for me." Tilly breezed in through the front door in a waft of expensive perfume.

"No; I was just going to bed." Alan kissed his daughter's cheek. "Had a good evening?"

"Yeah; Matty's cool." Matilda bounded up the stairs. "Night Dad; see you in the morning."

"Night night, Tilly." Alan switched off the porch light, turned the key in the Chubb lock, and thanked the good Lord that once again his daughter was home safe and sound.

Making sure to send Matthew home early the following afternoon and lock up in time, Alan drove eastwards out of the industrial estate: *He hated doctor's surgeries; all that waiting around in a room full of people hacking and spluttering. You always came out with more than you went in with.....*

However, on arrival he was pleased to see that just for once the surgery was surprisingly empty. He was called in almost straight away, and with a rising uneasiness he explained his symptoms as the locum peered at his neck with interest. After a brief examination the doctor remained silent for a time, which increased Alan's anxiety even further. Eventually, Doctor Gupta tossed a remark carelessly over his shoulder as he washed his hands at the sink.

"Regarding your comments, I don't think it's anything to do with your Adam's apple."

Alan was intelligent enough to have a heartsink moment at the implication of the doctor's words. Avoiding the question he really wanted to ask, he made his voice sound as unconcerned as possible.

"Er… what do you think it could be then?"

Dr Gupta dried his hands on a towel and turned back towards his desk:

"It could be a cyst on your thyroid, or possibly a small goitre. However, I would not be doing my job properly if I don't mention to you the very small possibility that it could be thyroid cancer. I'm going to refer you to Doctor Levine, the endocrinologist up at the hospital, and he'll investigate further for you; is that okay?"

"Sure." Relieved, Alan felt a growing certainty that the lump was a cyst.

"What do you do for a living?" The doctor started tapping letters on his computer keyboard.

"I'm a car mechanic; self-employed. I have my own garage on the Wynwright Industrial Estate."

"I see." The doctor continued typing. "I'll send a referral, and you'll receive an appointment to see Doctor Levine in due course."

"Thanks." Alan stood up and shook the doctor's hand.

He tried to appear nonchalant as he turned his key in the lock.

"Where have you been, Dad? Working late? I've made you some dinner." Matilda appeared in the hallway and smiled.

"Thanks; I'm starving. Sorry, I forgot to leave you a note. No; I've been to the doctors; he thinks I may have a cyst in my neck. I've got to see someone at the hospital about it." Alan smiled at his daughter and shrugged off the symptoms.

"Wow! Let's have a look then!" Matilda came nearer and peered at his neck.

"It's nothing really; just a little lump. They'll see to it at the hospital I expect." Alan pointed to the swelling.

"When have you got to go and have it taken out?" "I don't know; I've got to wait for an appointment." Her curiosity satisfied, Matilda shrugged her shoulders. "It looks like a cyst. Anyway; come and have your dinner. I've grilled some burgers."

"Burgers? That's not a dinner!"

"It is tonight; I haven't had time to go shopping."

"Burgers it is then."

# CHAPTER 5

"HOW ARE YOU with changing the crankshaft bearings on that Mondeo?" Alan wiped his hands on an oily rag and looked over with a *soupcon* of irritation at Matthew, his genial apprentice.

*If only Tilly hadn't finished college early on that Friday afternoon last July and popped in for a chat. If only he'd given Matthew a half day's holiday, then the greatest romance of the century might never have happened. As it was, he, Alan, was powerless to stop it, and his apprentice looked like having a better than average chance of becoming his son-in-law at this rate. With his luck the way it was at the moment, Matty would soon have his size 12 hobnails stuck firmly under the kitchen table, with maybe even a view to slowly edging his father-in-law out of his own business.....*

"No probs. I'll do it after lunch." Matthew, irritatingly as happy-go-lucky as ever, gave him the thumbs up before dipping his hands in a tub of Swarfega.

"After that I'll get you to help me change the clutch on that Ford Focus."

"Righty ho; I'm just going to phone Tilly now and have my sarnies."

"Can you ask her to pop into the supermarket after college? We're running out of stuff. I've got too much work on here to do it."

"Okay."

*What are you going to whisper in my daughter's ear, you scheming little toe-rag?*

Alan continued working through his lunch break. He'd had the Focus for far too long; the customer was beginning to complain, and was threatening to take the work to another garage. To keep the customer sweet, he would have to charge mates' rates and take a loss in profits. When the phone rang in the office, he signalled for Matthew to take the call, and carried on replacing some brake pads.

"It's for you Alan. It's the hospital; they want to speak to you." Matthew beckoned him over with a mouth full of cheese sandwich.

Alan knew what the call would be about. With the workload as it was at the moment, he could not even begin to consider attending the appointment. He walked to the little office at the back of the garage, and picked up the phone.

"Hello." He spoke confidently into the receiver.

"Mr Beaumont?"

"Yes."

"This is the Wynwright hospital's appointments department."

"Yes?" His voice carried just the right amount of impatience. *Get on with it!*

"We're calling to offer you an appointment to see Dr Levine this coming Thursday afternoon at half past two."

"No way can I attend that; I've got too much work on." He checked the time on his watch as he spoke.

"Dr Gupta wanted you to be seen urgently."

The female voice on the other end was polite and courteous. However, Alan had picked up on the sudden pressing need for him to be seen by a specialist. Alarm bells started ringing in his brain.

"Urgently? Why?"

"I'm not medically trained Mr Beaumont; I'm just ringing to offer you the next available appointment."

"Anything for late Friday afternoon instead?"

"We have a cancellation at twenty past four."

"Okay; I'll come to that one then."

"Please bring a list of your medication with you. I've booked you in for Friday at four twenty."

"Thanks, and I don't take any tablets."

Alan replaced the receiver. He could see Matthew outside on the forecourt still on his lunch break, and continuing to talk on his mobile phone. *The bugger had better not be interrupting Tilly's college work!* When the regulation half an hour had expired, Alan stuck the index and ring fingers of his right hand in his mouth and whistled loudly in the apprentice's direction.

"Oy! I'm not paying you to gas on the phone all bloody day!" He indicated his left thumb towards a shabby-looking Ford Mondeo.

"Coming!" Matthew gave him a wave, ended his call, and put his phone back in the top pocket of his overalls.

"You can go home early on Friday; I've got to lock up about four o'clock." Alan took a sip of cold tea and ignored the rumblings in his stomach.

"Ta; yeah, Tilly just told me about the lump in your neck. Are you seeing the specialist on Friday then?" Matthew looked at Alan with interest as he lifted up the Mondeo's bonnet.

Alan glared at Matthew with some degree of annoyance; *the boy was beginning to get on his tits!*

"Yeah." His hands bunched into fists again under the Fiesta's wheel arch, and his jaw clenched in anger.

"Good luck; hope it goes well for you." Matthew smiled and nodded before bending over the opened bonnet.

"Ta."

Alan wondered what else his daughter had gabbled on about. Did the boy now know that Tilly's mother had run off with the man that had once cleaned moss from their roof? Had the pair of them been discussing his neck lump at lunchtime? He would have to remind Tilly to keep all family business private.

# CHAPTER 6

DR LEVINE LOOKED over the top of his spectacles and stood up.

"Mr Beaumont! Come in; come in!" He waved a hand towards an empty chair.

"Ta; I've come about the cyst." Alan sat down nervously.

"Let me see now." The doctor moved his glasses back up the bridge of his nose, and glanced at a buff-coloured folder. "Your GP has referred you for investigations regarding a lump in your neck."

"Yeah."

"How long has it been there?" The consultant peered over at the swelling."

"Don't know Doc; I only noticed it a few weeks back when I was looking at myself in a mirror." Alan shrugged his shoulders and tipped his head up for the doctor to get a better view.

"I'll feel around the lump if I may?"

"Go ahead; it's not painful or anything."

Alan endured the unpleasant sensation of probing fingers around the front of his windpipe.

"Mr Beaumont; we'll need to find out the cause of this lump, so I'll book you in for an ultrasound scan and fine needle biopsy of the cyst. Also we'll need to take some blood to check your thyroid is working properly, and we'll also need some urine from you for testing."

"What's a urine test got to do with anything in my neck?" Alan gave a *tut* of annoyance.

"We have to check for the rare possibility that it might be thyroid cancer instead of a cyst. I'm sure you would agree that all avenues need to be investigated." Dr Levine jotted down a few notes as he spoke.

"Give us a test tube then, and I'll do the necessary." Alan looked around the room for a suitable receptacle: "Let's get it over with."

"I'm afraid it isn't as simple as that. The urine needs to be collected over a 24 hour period. You can start in the morning, and bring the containers back to us on Monday morning."

"Containers? Jeez! You mean I've got to piddle in a pot all the weekend?" Alan sighed at the thought of it.

"I'm afraid so. We must test the urine for thyroid cancer. I must do my job properly." Dr Levine managed a small smile.

"How can I do mine when I've got to walk around with two bottles of piss?"

"We need to run the tests, but you are at liberty to opt out if you so wish."

Alan could tell the doctor was becoming irritable. "Okay; I'll go along with it. Do I bring the containers back to you on Monday?"

"No; collect and return them to Pathology next door. Please give the receptionist there this ticket." The doctor wrote on a yellow prescription pad, tore off the top piece of paper, and held it at arm's length.

"Thanks; is that all?" Alan took the ticket and stood up.

"For now. We'll send you another appointment in a month or so when we have the results of all the tests."

On arriving home and turning the key in the lock, Alan glanced down the hallway into the kitchen and experienced a feeling of sadness at seeing his daughter standing at the table and rolling out pastry in that confident way that women have, and looking exactly like a younger version of her mother.

"You're home quicker than I thought; what did the doctor say? What are those containers for?" Matilda sprinkled flour onto the table, picked up the dough, and rolled it in the flour.

"They're for piddling in. What a palaver it all is; I wish I'd never gone there now." Alan rolled his eyes and put the containers on the table next to the pastry.

"Ewwww………get them off the table!   I'm making a pie!" Matilda wrinkled her nose.

"I haven't pissed in them yet; they're clean. Oh, and another thing; Matthew doesn't need to know all this. It's my business, so keep him out of it."

"Ooh… touchy today aren't we? Never mind Daddy, I've made your favourite for dinner; steak and kidney pie."

His daughter's infallible good humour annoyed him even more.

"That pie's too big for the two of us." Alan glowered at the size of it.

"Er… well, Matty's coming to dinner. Hope you don't mind, but I invited him because we're going off to see his brother tonight after dinner and staying over for the weekend."

"Where does his brother live?" Alan's heart sank at the latter five words.

"Brighton." Matilda expertly covered pieces of cooked steak and kidney with a layer of rolled out dough, and cut off the excess pastry around the pie tin with a knife.

"Does he live with their parents then?" Alan asked hopefully.

"No; he's gay; he lives with his boyfriend." Matilda kept her eyes on the pie tin.

"Where will you be sleeping?" Alan hoped his intuition was wrong.

"With Matty; we're a couple now." Matilda avoided his gaze, opened the oven door, and put the pie in.

Alan suddenly wished that Tina was around, even though she had caused him so much heartache.

"Tilly………"

"Dad, I'm eighteen; I'm all grown up. Don't worry, I won't be getting pregnant; for your information I've been taking the contraceptive pill for some time now."

At least his daughter had the decency to blush. Alan felt impotent, and helpless in the face of Tilly's revelations.

"I hope he's treating you well." He clung to a last vestige of hope.

"Like a princess; just like you do. I love him Dad, and he loves me."

*That was it; his innocent, beautiful girl was gone for good. He would just have to get on with it.*

"Have a nice time." He picked up the containers from the table and took them into the toilet.

# CHAPTER 7

"MRS MASON…."

"Ms."

"Ms Mason; I'll need you to keep perfectly still for the ultrasound and fine needle biopsy."

"Okay"

The radiologist hovered over her on the couch, and made her feel even more nervous than she was already.

"I'll just put some gel on your neck so that we can get a better picture."

The gel was cold on her skin, and the probe pushed down rather too forcefully on the front of her neck. Erin closed her eyes and thought about sitting in a deckchair and eating strawberries and cream in the sunshine. The probe moved from side to side. She could hear the radiologist's breathing in the silence of the room, as he scrutinised the screen in front of him.

"Actually, I'm not going to bother doing the biopsy, because I can see the whole of your thyroid is covered in cysts, rather than just one bit of it. You have what's known as a multi-nodular goitre. It is a benign condition. My advice is to have regular check-ups, but to leave it alone."

"Oh. Is that it? Can I go now?"

"That's it."

A nurse wiped the gel from her neck, and Erin sat up.

"Thanks very much." She gave a great sigh of relief, and grinned from ear to ear.

A week later she felt a lot happier when knocking on the endocrinologist's door.

"Good afternoon Ms Mason, do come in."

Erin noticed Dr Levine was all smiles as she sat herself down.

"Now; we've had all the results back from the blood and urine tests and the ultrasound scan. Your thyroid is covered in cysts, but it is working normally. As this is a non-cancerous condition we will just keep an eye on it and call you in for a check-up twice a year."

"So I haven't got cancer then?" She felt like dancing around the room.

"No. The radiologist's report diagnosed a multi-nodular goitre. I'll make an appointment for you to come back and see me again in six months, just to make sure the cysts haven't got any bigger."

"Thanks Dr Levine. You've put my mind at ease." She grinned away like a Cheshire cat.

"My pleasure. See you again later in the year."

Kieran rushed past her as she stood in the hallway in her dressing gown.

"Hi Mum! Thanks Dad! Great match!" He ran upstairs. "Bags I first in the shower!"

"Hi Mum."

"Hey Kevin; did you have a good weekend?" She gave him a hug.

"Yeah; Rooney scored a great goal in the second half!"

She smiled at her son as he disappeared into the kitchen in his usual quest for food, and then turned her attention towards her ex-husband.

"You're late bringing them back. They've got college tomorrow."

"London to Old Trafford isn't exactly around the corner, and *you* try getting out of Manchester after a match. The roads were closed off for ages, and we just sat there in the traffic. Marie's already given me a bollocking for keeping Freddie up, so I don't need another one, ta." He was instantly on the defensive.

"Couldn't you have come out earlier?"

She noticed his look of utter incredulity.

"Give over! Who comes out of a United match before it's finished? Anyway, what's this all about you having a lump? Kevin told me." He looked down at her neck.

"I've got some sort of goitre. I saw the endocrinologist again last Friday; he said it's nothing to worry about and all my tests are clear. I've had a scan and it's just a cyst."

"Good news, then." He smiled as he walked back down the garden path. "I'll pick up the boys again on Saturday week.

"Okay, but bring them back on time!"

With a wave of his hand he was gone, and Erin heard the car start up as she locked the front door. She thought back briefly to ten years' before when they had both been on the same side of the door, but as past happy family memories tended to make her a little on the depressed side, she quickly sloughed them off and strode into the kitchen to try to dissuade her young son from eating her out of house and home.

# CHAPTER 8

"MR BEAUMONT; COME in, come in!"

Alan sat down heavily in the chair. The possible outcome of all his tests had been hanging over him like a black cloud, along with his daughter's blatant new sexuality. He tried to gauge the doctor's expression, but the consultant was playing his cards very close to his chest.

"Mr Beaumont; how have you been since we last met?" Dr Levine peered over the top of his rimless spectacles.

"Fine; overworked as usual, but no symptoms from the lump or anything." Alan tried to read the computer screen, but it was tilted at the wrong angle.

"We've had the results back from your biopsy and from the blood and urine tests. Your thyroid is working perfectly normally and you have a normal full blood count…"

"Well, that's great then isn't it?" Alan felt relief wash over him.

"Unfortunately though, the ultrasound scan showed abnormalities, and the needle biopsy from different areas of your thyroid showed that cancerous cells are present. We recommend that you are referred to an endocrine surgeon to have your thyroid gland removed surgically, and from there on referred to an oncologist for treatment and monitoring of the cancer."

The black cloud threatened to envelop him altogether. Alan stared uncomprehendingly at the consultant.

"Cancer? You say I've got cancer?" He thought of his daughter and wanted to cry.

"Thyroid cancer often hits in middle age, but responds very well to treatment. At this moment in time there is no cause for concern." Dr Levine smiled encouragingly at his patient.

"Well, how the hell have I got it?" Alan shook his head in disbelief.

"There are a few unproven theories; the fallout from Chernobyl, or with women it could be caused by the sudden weight gain and weight loss during pregnancy and childbirth. For men and women, maybe if they've had lots of dental x-rays. We don't really know, so these are just guesses." Dr Levine held out the palms of his hands and lifted his shoulders.

"I've definitely had many, many dental x-rays; enough to make quite a big pile." Alan sighed and wondered how to sue his dentist.

"As I say, there's no proven theory. It's a difficult cancer to find a cause for."

"So what's next for me, Doc?" Alan, slumped in his chair, felt the weight of the world was upon his shoulders.

"A referral to our endocrine surgeon Mr Barker-Lomax. You'll receive an appointment to see him in clinic prior to your surgery, where you can discuss any concerns you may have regarding the operation."

"Is it a long operation?" Alan wondered how much time he would need to take off work.

"Unfortunately it is a major operation, and could take three or four hours. However, Mr Barker-Lomax is an experienced surgeon. You will need to take time off work to recover afterwards, and also for the radioiodine treatment that will certainly follow. You will also need to be on a lifelong thyroxine replacement, but the oncologist will guide you through that side of it."

"I'm self-employed! If I don't work, I don't get paid." Alan wondered what terrible thing he might have done in the past to be punished so hard.

"Do you have anybody working for you who could take over while you recover?" Doctor Levine enquired hopefully.

Alan nodded silently. His fears, previously ungrounded, were now proving to be real.

*The bastard had taken his daughter, and now he would be taking over his job!*

# CHAPTER 9

"CALL THE FOUR ones; we've got a cardiac arrest in bay five!"

Pressing the number one button on the phone four times, she was instantly connected to the hospital switchboard.

"Emergency; Somerset ward. Bay five. Cardiac arrest." She kept her voice even.

"Okay, I'll bleep the Resuss team."

Within minutes the heavy main doors flew open as the Resuss team charged in at full pelt, breathless and fuelled on adrenaline.

"Bay five!"

Erin pointed towards the end bay, as the team, frantic and unseeing, immediately ran to Bay one at the opposite end. Too late, she remembered that Someset ward was the only ward in the hospital with its five bays arranged back to front. Throwing down her pen she ran along the corridor to head them off and send them back running in the other direction. She caught a whiff of stale sweat as the team rushed past, intent in their mission.

*Christ! It's like the Keystone cops in this place!*

"Erin, can you do the menus today for bays three, four and five please? They're a bit short-staffed." Staff Nurse Miller appeared at the desk, as welcome as a blizzard in August.

"Yes, Staff."

Sighing with the knowledge of what was coming next, she picked up her pen and a wad of blank menus and made her way to the first bed in bay three, reluctantly giving over her seat to a hovering care co-ordinator, who jumped at the chance of being able to use *her* computer to update one of the discharge summaries:

"Good morning Ethel. What would you like for lunch today?"

The ancient face looked up at her uncomprehendingly. "What?"

"I said good morning, and what would you like for lunch?" Erin raised her voice a little and moved in closer.

"You'll have to shout; I'm a bit deaf."

"Lunch! What do you want?" Her voice sounded a trifle hoarse as she began to shout.

"What have you got?" Ethel took a menu from Erin's outstretched hand. "I've lost my glasses; you'll have to read it."

"Ham sandwiches and soup, jacket potato, or salad?" "What?"

"Ham sandwiches and soup, jacket potato, or salad!" Her voice broke like an adolescent schoolboy's.

"Ham sandwiches please. I don't want any soup."

"Brown bread or white?"

"What?"

"Brown or white!"

"White."

"Thank you Ethel."

She moved on to the second bed.

"Morning Betty. What would you like for lunch?"

"Pardon?" Betty cupped a hand to her ear.

"I'm here to find out what you want for lunch!" She shouted out loud enough to be heard in the next bay.

"Oh, anything dear; I don't mind."

"Sandwiches?"

"What?"

"Do you like sandwiches?"

"No."

"What about a jacket potato?"

"Pardon?" Betty cupped a hand to her ear again.

"Jacket potatoes!" Her voice was definitely becoming hoarse, and there were still another 16 patients to go.

"No, I don't want to wear a jacket."

"Soup?"

"No, I haven't done a poop. I haven't been for three days!"

"Your voice is different tonight, Mum." Kevin took a large bite out of his beefburger.

"Yeah; you sound like Kev did when his voice was breaking." Kieran helped himself to more salad.

"I didn't sound like that!" Kevin chewed his burger as he spoke.

"Kevin; I don't want to see that burger going around inside your mouth like a cement mixer." Erin put down her knife and fork. "I'm just a bit hoarse today that's all. I had to do eighteen menus, and the patients were all deaf except one."

"What?"

"Half past twelve."

"Don't you two start as well!" She could not help but grin at the pair of them.

It was only shortly after that when, unusually for her, she started sleeping badly. Try as she might, she could not get comfortable in bed; there seemed to be a feeling of pressure in her neck when she laid on one side, and she started to get choking feelings and had to cough frequently. She was not used to sleeping on her back, and most nights saw her creeping downstairs to sleep in a more comfortable propped-up position in one of the recliner armchairs. When she found herself losing interest at work due to over-tiredness, she decided to phone the Appointments department and expedite her check-up with the endocrinologist.

# CHAPTER 10

"MS MASON! COME in!  How have you been?"

Erin shook Dr Levine's outstretched hand as he stood up to greet her.

"That's why I've come back to see you a bit earlier than planned. I've got a feeling the cysts might be getting bigger. I can feel something in my neck when I lay on my side in bed. I'm having trouble sleeping."

"Hmm; any problems breathing or swallowing?" He took his seat again, motioned for her to sit down, and swivelled his chair around to face her.

"No, but I get a choking feeling sometimes and it makes my eyes water and I have to cough."

"Hmm; the choking feeling sounds rather non-specific. Let me have a look at the lump though."

He prodded around the hollow at the base of her neck, while Erin closed her eyes and thought about two adorable red-headed toddlers sitting between her and Chris on the beach eating chocolate ice cream cones.

"I think we'll have another ultrasound scan if that's alright with you? I'm going to request one now." He pressed a few buttons and logged into his computer.

"Yes, I think that's a good idea." She dragged herself back from the long-ago happy family scene with reluctance.

"You'll receive an appointment soon, and also another one to come back and see me to discuss the results."

"Thank you, doctor. I'd better get back to work now." She stood up and shook his hand again.

The stench of a ripe farmyard greeted her as she opened the door to the ward.

"'Elp me darlin'!" Tommy Beale stood at her desk proffering a set of gleamingly white gnashers.

"Are you back in again Tommy? But whose teeth are these?" She put down her bag and placed her jacket over *her* chair to claim it.

"Can you 'elp me, darlin'?"

"Are these your teeth?" Erin took the full set of dentures from Tommy's hand, and scrutinised the lower part of his face. "No, I can see you've got yours in. Where did you find them?" She held the teeth up in front of him.

"'Elp me, darlin', 'elp me."

"I thought we'd already decided I'm not your darling. Now, whose bedside cabinet did you take the teeth from?"

The old man looked at her with a blank expression on his face. Erin sighed as she looked around for a plastic bag in which to store them until claimed by their rightful gummy owner.

"You're a naughty boy, Tommy. You shouldn't go

around taking what doesn't belong to

you." "'Elp me, 'elp me."

"How did you get on with Mr Hormone?"

Erin looked up from the computer at Trixie after processing the new arrivals.

"Okay: I've got to have another scan."

"Oh, poor you."

"I see we've got Tommy and Dennis in again."

"Yeah; Dennis had two bottles of whisky in his bag when we did the property list. He was as high as a kite when he came in last night. Watch out for the rellies though; they'll be bringing in more probably.

"How wicked is that?" Erin shook her head. "He was yellow enough the last time."

"He phones them up and pays them over the odds to bring it in. We'll dry him out temporarily and send him on his way; it's all we can do." Trixie shrugged her shoulders. "Let me know how you get on with your scan." She smiled and turned towards bay 4. "Oh God, do you want to do the honours or shall I?" She indicated a finger towards the second bed, where Ernest Williams lay asleep on top of the bedclothes, open-mouthed, and with his penis laying at a jaunty angle outside the front opening of his stripy pyjamas.

"At least it's not sticking out! Find a pair of tongs and poke it back in. With a bit of luck he won't wake up." Erin chuckled as she wrinkled her nose up.

"I'm not sure it's in my job description!" Trixie's shrill laugh echoed down the corridor.

"I *know* it's definitely not in mine, thank goodness!" Erin grinned and looked down at the computer again to block out the sight.

# CHAPTER 11

"WE MEET AGAIN Ms Mason! Come in and sit down."

Nervously seating herself in the only available chair, Erin smiled at the duty nurse and then looked hopefully at the endocrinologist.

"Hello, Dr Levine. I take it you have the latest ultrasound results?"

"Yes." He put on his glasses and looked at the computer screen. "The scan shows some of the cysts have grown a bit bigger…..."

The doctor paused and Erin wondered what was coming next.

"Er……the condition has progressed, and I feel that probably surgery would be the better option to prevent interference to breathing and swallowing mechanisms."

She let the information sink in for a moment before replying.

"Do you mean I'm going to need an operation?" She felt slightly panicky, and twiddled a longer piece of her layered auburn hair round and round on her finger.

"I'm afraid so; a total thyroidectomy would be in your best interests I think."

"What's that?" She tried to concentrate on her toddlers eating ice cream again, but the reality of her situation kept coming to the fore.

"Surgical removal of your thyroid gland. After this you would see me for regular checks on your thyroxine levels, the hormone in tablet form that you will have to take for the rest of your life to compensate for the loss of your thyroid." The doctor took off his glasses and rubbed them with a nearby clean cloth.

"Oh God! I've never had an operation before! The only time I've been an in-patient was when I had the twins." She felt like crying at the thought of it.

"It is a major operation; you'll need to take about three weeks off work to recover afterwards, but if you take a daily tablet of thyroxine afterwards you will be able to lead a normal life." The doctor smiled. "If you are in agreement I will refer you urgently to an endocrine surgeon, ah.........probably Mr Barker-Lomax, who will send you an appointment to see him in clinic prior to the operation." "Are there no other options?" She grasped at the last straw as though clinging to a life raft adrift in a stormy sea.

"The whole gland is growing bigger. Sooner or later you will not be able to breathe or swallow. I am going to recommend that the surgery takes place quite soon."

"Mr Barker-Lomax it is then." She sighed. "If he can possibly schedule it during the summer holidays, then my boys can stay with their father while I recover."

"I will suggest the surgery takes place in August when I dictate my letter."

"Boys; I've got to go into hospital, but by then college will be out for the summer. You'll have to stay with Dad and Marie for a while until I've recovered." Erin swallowed a piece of chicken and waited for the response.

"What's the matter with you?" Kevin was instantly concerned, while Kieran put down his knife and fork and listened intently.

"I've got to have my thyroid gland taken out." She pointed to the front of her neck. "Nan will stay here for a few weeks to help me, and after that when I'm fit again you can come home."

"I want to help you. I don't want to stay with Dad!" Kevin looked close to tears.

"Marie can't cook like you." Kieran's face was grim. "It'll only be for a few weeks. Dad was taking you on holiday anyway. Don't worry, I'll be fighting fit again in no time at all."

The boys were quiet and seemed extra helpful after dinner, washing and drying up without complaint. Erin drove them to their youth club, and after coming back home she flopped onto the settee to try and get her head around the situation. In the end she decided there was only one thing to do, and picked up the phone:

"Hello?"

"Marie, this is Erin. Could I speak to Chris please?" "Oh; sure. Hang on, I'll get him. No Freddie, it's not for you."

She took advantage of the moment to clear her throat. "Erin?"

"Hi Chris. I'm afraid I need to ask you a favour."

"What?" His voice still sounded the same, even after ten years.

"I've got to have a major operation soon. I'll hang on until college is out, but the boys will have to stay with you for a few weeks until I'm fit again."

"Oh? What's wrong? Tell me it's none of my business if you like though."

*She wanted to shout out that of course it was his business — didn't they used to love each other? Didn't they once promise to love and to cherish each other until being parted by death instead of divorce?*

"My thyroid's got to come out. Apparently it's a big op. I'll get Mum over to help, but it would be better if I haven't got to cope with the boys as well."

"Of course. We're taking them to Wales for a fortnight on holiday anyway. They can stay with us after as well, until college starts again if you like."

"Well, thanks, although I hope I'll be fighting fit again by then. I just thought I'd let you know sooner rather than later."

"Thanks for letting me know."

*Is that all you're going to say?*

"Bye then."

"Bye."

# CHAPTER 12

ERIN SAT IN the ward manager's office and nervously crossed and re-crossed her legs.

"I've been referred urgently to Mr Barker-Lomax for a thyroidectomy. I haven't had an appointment yet, but as it's a big operation I'm going to need three weeks off work. Sorry; I know it'll coincide with the new junior doctors coming in, but I have no choice; I've got to have it done."

"Ooh, thyroids can be nasty! We'll be sorry to lose you for a while, but as with all employees, your health has to come first. Get better and come back to work when you've recovered. I'll ask one of the healthcare assistants to take over ward clerking until you return." Lisa Monroe smiled sympathetically.

"Thanks Lisa." Erin smiled and stood up. "I'll definitely be here for the rest of the week though, and probably next week as well."

"Just let me know when you get a date."

"Will do."

The usual essence of faeces hit Erin in the face like a smack as she strode back into the ward. The phone was ringing incessantly, and to her irritation it was being ignored *again* by everyone sitting at the desk, including Madeleine, the large staff nurse who was slumped in *her* chair. A bed on castors was taking up a substantial part of the front reception area on the other side of the desk. Erin looked past the porter waiting to hand over the patient, to the wizened occupant in the bed who gazed sadly back at her.

"New patient from Emergency Admissions. You'll have to make up some notes from scratch, because we don't know who she is. Somebody dumped her in A&E this morning and legged it." The porter whispered conspiratorially to Erin.

"Poor thing! Hasn't anybody asked her what her name is?"

"Yeah, but you get a different answer every time. At the moment she's the Queen of Sheba, but keeps saying that she's one hundred and two on October the fifteenth, which seems to be consistent with each previous answer though."

"There's room in bay one down the end." She pointed towards the double doors at the end of the corridor. "I'll ask Trixie to do a property check."

"There's no property. They left her sitting in a wheelchair in A&E. Nice family." The porter rolled his eyes upwards as he began to push the bed towards the first bay.

Erin could not wait to get Madeleine's lazy arse to move from *her* chair.

"Are you looking after bay one today, Maddy?"

"No; I'm in bays three, four and five."

*No you're not, you are in my seat! Move your fucking arse, you lazy cow!*

"Who's in charge of bay one today then?"

"Have a look at the off-duty. I think it might be Yvonne, but she's on her break." Madeleine sighed and stood up. "Shit; I suppose I'd better start the medicines now." Her large frame rose to its feet and waddled towards the drugs trolley.

"I'll see if I can find out the old lady's name anyway." Erin put a pile of discharged patients' notes onto *her* chair to dissuade anybody else from sitting in it, and made her way down the corridor to bay one.

"Hello! My name's Erin. I'm the ward clerk. What's your name?"

"What?" A thin, quavery voice emanated from the bed.

"What's your name?"

"I'm the Queen of Sheba."

"Hello Queenie. What's your date of birth?"

"Pardon?"

"When were you born?" Erin's voice cracked as she shouted a bit louder.

"October the fifteenth, nineteen eleven. I'll be a hundred and two this year."

"Can I call you Queenie?" She shouted the question to save time.

"No. What do you want to call me Queenie for?" The old woman looked at her with gimlet eyes.

"Because you're the Queen of Sheba."

"Eh?"

"Are you the Queen of Sheba?" Erin yelled as loudly as she could manage.

"Of course not! I'm Florence Maude Lillistone, 12 Park Gardens."

Erin was taken aback at the sudden lucidity.

"I'll tell staff nurse you're here, and go and find your notes."

"When am I going home? My son will be wondering where I am."

Erin remained non-committal as she took a moment to wonder regarding the age of the old lady's son and whether he had been at his wits' end; dumping his mother out of desperation for a little bit of peace and quiet in his own declining years. She could see another caseload building for the already overworked Social Services Department.

"Ms Mason; I've examined your neck, and I agree with Dr Levine that a thyroidectomy would be wise. However, it is my duty to tell you of the possible complications of the operation before you sign the consent form."

"Thanks Mr Barker-Lomax, but I don't think I want to know." Erin wanted to think of her babies, warm and fed, asleep for a Sunday afternoon nap in their twin pram, while she and Chris made delicious love on the settee in the front room.

"I have to tell you of possible pain, bleeding and infection, inadvertent damage to one or both of your vocal cords, and possible damage or removal of your parathyroid glands."

"I'll sign the form now if you don't mind." She took a pen from her bag.

"Very well. You will receive an appointment to attend the pre-assessment clinic, where you will be swabbed for MRSA, and also have your heart rate, temperature, blood pressure and urine checked. Have you any dental problems? Cracked teeth? Anything like that?"

"Not that I know of."

"We'll see you soon.  I've put you on the urgent waiting list."

"Thanks; I think." Erin shook his hand while her heart sank to the bottom of her boots.

"Are you sure you don't want me to stay?"

She finished helping Kevin pack his rucksack, shook her head, and gave him a hug.

"I'm fine. Have a lovely holiday and I'll see you when I'm recovered from the op." She smiled at him. "Dad will be here in a minute to collect you. Where's Kieran's stuff?"

"By the front door. He's busy in the garden saying goodbye to his bird."

"His girlfriend's in the garden?"

"No; I mean he's on the phone in the garden so we can't hear."

"Oh: Is it still Denise?"

"I think so, but he's a bit cagey at the moment. When have you got to go into hospital?"

"Monday morning at eight o'clock."

"Can I phone you on Monday night?"

"You can, but I don't know if I'll be answering. I expect Nan would have phoned me twenty times by then, so you might want to ring her for an update."

"But then she'll never stop talking at all."

"She can't help it; she lives on her own."

"No wonder."

"Don't be mean!"

"Sorry.  Love you."

"Love you too.  I think I can hear Dad's car outside."

She followed her son downstairs and opened the front door, noticing that Kieran stopped chatting on his phone as soon as they appeared in the garden.

"Bye Mum. Hope the op goes okay."

"Bye Kieran. Thanks. Have a great holiday, and see you in a few weeks." She gave him a hug as she saw Chris get out of the car and wave.

"Let me know if you need anything!"

"Thanks Chris." She waved back to her ex-husband as the boys approached the car. "Whose turn is it to sit in the front?"

"We don't care about that anymore." Kevin turned around and waved.

"Yeah; we're all grown up." Kieran turned away from her and looked at his phone as it beeped with an incoming text.

She forced a smile, and waved at them through a sudden sea of mist behind her eyes.

# CHAPTER 13

"DON'T CRY LOVE; I'm not going to die. The doc says it can be treated." Alan cuddled Tilly, who wept inconsolably.

"Mum's gone; you can't leave me as well!" Tilly threw her arms around her father's neck and howled.

"I'm not going anywhere. I just need an operation to clear it, and then I'll be as good as new."

"Matty's been working for you for five years now; he can take over while you're in hospital." Tilly hiccupped and sighed.

"That's what I'm afraid of!" Alan chuckled and tried to make light of the situation.

"You never give him enough responsibility." Tilly's words came in short sobs as she wiped her eyes. "He says he can do everything you do; he must be a fully-fledged mechanic by now."

"You're right, love; I know I've been holding him back. He passed all his college exams with flying colours. He's a good lad." Alan held his daughter tight and suddenly realised he was going to need the boy's help like never before.

"Good; can I tell him everything then? He's coming to pick me up later."

"I suppose so; we can't really get out of *not* telling him can we?" Alan rolled his eyes to the heavens as he comforted his daughter and rested the bottom of his chin on her head. "If he's to run the garage on his own for a few weeks, you can tell him there'll be an increase in his pay packet." He added grudgingly.

"Thanks; he'll love that. When are you going in hospital?" Tilly sniffed and blew her nose.

"Don't know yet. I've got to wait for an appointment to see the surgeon."

Matilda unclasped her hands from around her father's neck and took a deep breath.

"Sorry for being such a wuss; it was just a bit of a shock, that's all. It won't happen again."

"No worries, love; it was a shock for me as well!" Alan smiled at his daughter. "How's it going with God's Gift?"

"Mind your own biz!" Tilly raised an index finger to the tip of her nose. "Okay; very well if you want to know. And no, I'm not pregnant yet either."

"The thought was never further from my mind." Alan lied and chuckled again.

"Liar." Tilly smiled shyly and picked up her phone. "I'll text Matty to come over earlier and we can all sit down together."

"Marvellous." Alan switched on the TV and tried to blot out the forthcoming meeting from his mind.

Tilly jumped up like a scalded cat when the doorbell rang an hour later. Alan sat and wondered if the bank balance would buckle under the proposed pay rise for his newly-promoted employee.

"Cheers for the pay rise, Alan! Tilly's filled me in. Don't worry about anything; I'll keep the garage running like clockwork for you." Beaming, Matthew bounced into the front room.

"I know you'll manage; that's why I've taken you off apprentice wages. I suppose you've earned your pay rise." Alan smiled and wished he had as smooth and unblemished a neck as the young man had who was standing in front of him.

"Thanks so much; my old Mum can't stop smiling."

The boy's good humour was infectious. Alan found himself warming to the lad and even thinking to himself that plenty of fathers would probably give their eye teeth to see their daughters settled with somebody like Matthew.

*Perhaps he had been too harsh on the boy.......?*

After only three weeks of waiting for a letter to drop onto the mat, his heart missed a beat when eventually he held the appointment date in his hand. On the day of his meeting with the surgeon, Alan took a deep breath, said a quick prayer, and opened the door of the consulting room.

"Come in! How do you do? I'm Laurence Barker-Lomax" The surgeon held out his hand.

"Alan Beaumont." Alan grasped the extended manicured hand and shook it.

"Dr Levine referred you to me. I'm an endocrine surgeon; I remove thyroids for my sins."

Alan smiled.

"I've got one that needs to come out, as you probably already know."

The surgeon nodded his head.

"The sooner the better as far as I'm concerned. What say you?"

"Yes; let's get it over with." Alan settled himself in a comfortable chair. *Bring it on!*

"I have a little bit of a waiting list, but it's not too long. You'll probably be called in some time towards the end of August. We can talk about the operation today, I'll give you the risks and possible side-effects, and then I'll get you to sign the consent form. We'll biopsy the whole thyroid after the operation, and then I'll need to refer you on to Dr Ingram, the Oncologist, who will oversee your treatment after my surgery. Results of your needle biopsy are showing cells of papillary thyroid cancer; the most common form and the most easily treatable."

"That's good I suppose?" Alan shrugged.

"As good as it can be under the circumstances." The surgeon shuffled his notes. "I'll let Pre-assessment know about you, and they'll call you in for swabs and to meet the anaesthetist."

"Oh goody." Alan suddenly wished he could fast-forward his life.

# CHAPTER 14

"AND SHE SAID '*You never said that, did you?*', and I said '*God's honest truth, I did*', and she said '*I wish I'd been there!*"

Erin tried to ignore the verbal diarrhoea issuing from her mother's mouth. She had no idea who or what her mother was talking about. Cynthia Parry paused slightly to inhale, and then carried on before Erin could get a word in edgeways.

"And I said you should have been there because of the look on her face. It was like she'd been sucking lemons……"

"Mum….can you just drive and let me look out of the window? I'm not in the mood for much conversation at the moment."

"Sorry, I do rabbit on a bit, but I've got so much to tell you."

Erin closed her eyes and wished her mother would just concentrate on driving and *shut the fuck up!*

"You don't have to stay with me at the hospital. Just drop me off and pick me up again in a couple of days when I ring."

"Are you sure? I'd like to stay to make sure you're alright."

"There's a whole medical team to do that. Really, just drop me off; I'll be fine."

"Did I tell you about the pain in my right knee? It's keeping me awake at night."

Erin exhaled with vigour; *only about three thousand times………..*

"Perhaps you can see the GP?"

"Oh *him!* He's about as much use as a chocolate fireguard! No, I'm obviously meant to spend the rest of my life in pain."

Erin fought off the urge to open the car door and jump out while it was going along.

"Mum; you've been saying that since you were forty." *I've been listening to one or another of your pains for 28 years!*

"Me and pain; we walk hand in hand."

In the caged confines of the car, Erin felt trapped and unable to escape. Her mother's whining and wittering went in one ear and promptly out of the other. When the car eventually pulled up in front of the hospital's main doors, she breathed a silent sigh of relief.

"Thanks for the lift. I'll call you when I'm due to be discharged."

"Let me park the car and come in with you."

"No, honestly; I'll be fine." She gave her mother a quick peck on the cheek and reached for her bag.

"Good luck Erin; I hope it goes well for you. I'll be here as soon as you call."

"Okay, thanks." She felt guilty at dismissing her mother so abruptly, but needed to keep her stress level from rising any further than its current highly augmented status.

"Hey Bev, I'm here and ready!" She gave the ward clerk on Essex Surgical a thin smile, which belied the fact that her legs had turned to jelly.

"Hi Erin!  I'll let Eve know you're here."

She watched Bev walk off to find the staff nurse, and took a quick peek inside the female bay opposite, noticing how much younger the faces looked compared to the non-surgical patients on Somerset ward.

"Ms Mason, I'm staff nurse Evelyn Richards. If you follow me I'll show you to your bed. You'll be last on Mr Barker-Lomax's list this morning because we've had a couple of emergencies. He's currently operating on the first patient, but you shouldn't have too long to wait."

Erin walked with leaden feet behind the staff nurse as she quickly made her way to the one empty bed in the first bay.

"I'll let you get settled in and then one of our nurses will be along to do a property list and take a few details about next of kin and past medical history etcetera. When was the last time you ate or drank anything?"

"Last night about ten o'clock."

"That's fine. All your results from the pre-assessment clinic were normal, so it's all systems go. There's a gown at the bottom of your bed there to put on when you're ready, and some stockings to combat DVT." The staff nurse smiled as she drew the curtains around the bed. "How are you feeling?"

"Terrified!" Erin felt like crying.

"I'll ask the doctor to prescribe something for you that will help, but you'll need to get into bed once you've taken it." She smiled again. "Try not to worry. It'll all be over soon." She disappeared, leaving Erin clutching her bag and looking at her surroundings.

Due to ward similarities the bed, bedside cabinet and armchair seemed somehow familiar but strange at the same time. Erin unpacked her bag, took off her clothes, donned her gown and stockings, and then pulled back the curtains before getting into bed to await her fate. She could see the other occupants of the beds were all sound asleep, and so took a crossword puzzle book out of her bag to help pass the time.

"The porters are ready to take you to Theatre, Ms Mason."

Erin woke up from a doze, and was surprised to find the tranquiliser she had recently swallowed had taken effect without her realising it. She was still holding her crossword book, which was taken from her hands and placed on the bedside cabinet. Through a haze she saw two young men wearing uniform blue shirts taking hold of either end of her bed, and then felt the bed moving along out of the ward and down the corridor towards the operating theatre. She had seen colourful pictures of cartoon characters on the ceiling thousands of times, but never from her current position. She was aware of people looking at her as they passed her by in the corridor, and she realised she had been guilty of doing just the same thing in the course of her everyday journeys around the hospital. She closed her eyes and could hear the laughter of two red-haired toddlers as they splashed in the sea at Brighton. When the anaesthetist injected the liquid cosh through a cannula, he was surprised to see that the patient was calm and even had a faint smile upon her face.

# CHAPTER 15

SHE WAS SUDDENLY wide awake; wider awake than she had ever been. She could feel devices on her lower legs inflating and deflating at regular intervals, obviously helping out the stockings in their anti-DVT mission. Her heart was pounding in her chest, there was something stuck in her nose, and she was aware of an urgent need to pee. A disembodied voice sounded in her left ear.

"Erin, you're in Recovery now. There's an oxygen tube in your nose to help oxygenate your red blood cells; we'll leave it in there for a few hours. Do you feel sick?"

"No." Her voice came out as a whisper. "But I need a wee." She tried to move her head to the left, but could not.

"You've had a lot of fluids through the cannula, and it was a long operation. The nurses will help you onto a bedpan, and then the porters will take you back to the ward.

She felt as weak as a kitten. Closing her eyes against the dizziness, she blocked out the mortifying transfer to a bedpan, and hoped she would never come face to face with the Recovery nurses in the hospital corridors ever again.

"Sorry about this." She whispered to the nurses as she passed urine.

"It doesn't matter. Don't worry." The nurse was kindness personified.

She tried to cough to clear her throat of an increase in phlegm, but her ability to cough had vanished. She began to panic.

"Can I have some water please? I'm terribly thirsty." She felt out of breath while whispering and terrifyingly out of control of her body, but reasoned that some water on the back of her parched throat might help to bring her voice and coughing mechanism back.

"Just a sip. It's too early yet for a proper drink."

A disembodied hand moved around with a straw in a paper cup containing a miniscule amount of water. As Erin took a sip she started to choke.

"I can't cough! I'm choking!" She whispered frantically as she tried to dislodge the feeling of water going down her windpipe.

"Don't worry" said the voice, "It'll feel strange, but your swallowing will come back; just give it time. Your body has to readjust to the new normal."

She managed to swallow a tiny amount of water, then gave the paper cup back to the outstretched hand, who removed it along with a full bedpan. Her temperature, blood pressure and pulse were measured, and a pleasant nurse then stood in front of her who Erin realised was the owner of the disembodied voice:

"Your blood pressure and heart rate are a little bit raised. We're just going to do an ECG before we send you back to the ward."

"Am I going to have a heart attack?" As she wheezed and whispered, she wondered what on earth the surgeon had done to her.

"No, but you've had a major operation. It's a shock to the body, but you'll be fine; don't worry."

Reassured for the moment, Erin lay back on the pillow and closed her eyes to block out the sight of the ECG equipment. When she heard a doctor mention that he was unconcerned because her heart beat was regular, she relaxed a little bit more and thought back to the agreeable sight of Chris in his tight swimming trunks playing lifeguard on Brighton beach to their two toddlers who knew no fear.

"Hello Ms Mason, how are you feeling?"

Erin opened her eyes again to find a smiling Mr Barker-Lomax. She felt surgically raped and wanted to give him a piece of her mind, but felt too weak in her present state.

"I've no voice, and I can't cough." She whispered and tried to clear her throat again while thinking of a thousand ways to kill him by slow torture.

"Ms Mason; I need to tell you that unfortunately I strongly suspect neoplasms in the excised thyroid gland and surrounding tissue."

She looked at him uncomprehendingly for what seemed like an eternity. She saw the owner of the disembodied hand moving in closer to her colleague as if to reinforce his message.

"What?" She wheezed and tried to sit up.

"Ms Mason; I think your thyroid gland may be cancerous, but of course we will await the results of the biopsy for confirmation. However, I have performed many such operations, and it is my duty to tell you of my suspicions."

"No; I haven't got cancer. Dr Levine" (she found she had to stop and draw breath) "told me I have a multi-nodular goitre." As she whispered she started to panic at the length of time it took her to inhale.

"In my opinion, Ms Mason, there may be malignancy present. I will ask my secretary to send a follow up appointment for you to see me in two weeks' time so that I can check the scar has healed and go over the results of the biopsy with you." He gave her a slight smile. "As you are awake now you can be taken back to the ward."

"How long have I got left?" She heard her voice as though it was coming from another person.

"Don't worry; if you do have thyroid cancer it's often very treatable; it's one of the better cancers, if 'better' is the right word. The majority of patients eventually die of something else."

The doctor stood awkwardly in front of her before turning on his heel and exiting the Recovery suite. Erin decided to set her mind to the fact that it just might not be cancer, and tried to blot out what she had just heard. However, all she could think about to take her mind off the surgeon's revelation was coming home early from a day out with the boys and finding Chris in the sanctity of their marriage bed with Marie, and the look of utter surprise on both of their faces as she came into the room.

She turned her mind reluctantly to the present as the porters came to wheel her back along the corridor. The other five patients in the ward were all awake, sitting in bedside armchairs and chatting to their visitors. She was aware of their gaze and felt like an exhibit in a freak show. Trying unsuccessfully to move her neck, she spoke to the porters in a breathy whisper.

"Can you pull the curtains round, please?"

When the porters had gone she cried silently, glad of the curtained privacy the cubicle afforded. The nurses came in and out at regular intervals, checking her blood pressure and temperature, and giving her sips of water. She dreaded their efforts to make her drink. She was terrified of choking, and of the phlegm that kept building up in the back of her throat.

# CHAPTER 16

"WHY ARE THESE curtains closed?"

The nurse's strident tones woke Erin from a doze. She lifted her arm to check the time on her wristwatch; the hands showed nine o'clock. She realised the night shift had taken over.

"I wanted them shut." She whispered.

Staff Nurse Imbeah had a slightly abrupt manner and made a *tutting* noise as she sucked her teeth and pulled the curtains back.

"No good feeling sorry for yourself.    That won't do at all."

Erin gave the nurse a stare and felt like crying again at the woman's lack of sympathy. *Just see how you bloody well feel if you are ever given a diagnosis of cancer!*

"We'll get you up tomorrow for a little wash, but tonight it's best that you stay in bed. Do you need a bedpan?" The nurse fussed around the bedclothes, tucking in corners and smoothing the blankets.

"No."

"Your blood pressure and heart rate have come down nicely."

"I can't cough, and I've got loads of phlegm." Erin wheezed and tried to clear her throat.

"I'll get the doctor to prescribe some saline nebulisers for you to inhale. They'll help break it up. It was a long operation, and the anaesthetic gases cause the phlegm problem. You were on the table for three hours, you know." She consulted the notes that were clipped to the end of the bed. "I'll bleep the on-call doctor and he can write them up for you on your drug chart."

"Thanks."

"Don't look so grim. We have loads of thyroid cancer patients in here; it's treatable."

"So I've been told." *But I might not even have it anyway!*

"Would you like a little snack? Some toast?" "No thanks, just water."

"Are you in pain?"

"Not really."

"Well, that's good then. Have a few words with these lovely ladies in here for a while, and I'll pull the curtains round again when I turn off the main lights in an hour or so."

Erin's heart sank at the thought of having to converse with anybody else at that precise moment. When the night nurse walked away she closed her eyes and thought back to when she had been 26, healthy, and in the full bloom of her pregnancy.

"Hi; my name's Irene."

Erin was jolted back to reality by a voice emanating from the side of her bed. She opened her eyes, shifted her position, and gazed at the fifty-something woman standing over her.

"I've just had me left boob off. I could say I feel a right tit, but that one's gone as well."

"Breast cancer?" Erin smiled amidst the grimness of her situation.

"It's a bastard ain't it?" Irene smiled back. "It won't beat me though."

"I'm Erin. The doctor thinks I may have thyroid cancer." Erin whispered as fast as she could before she ran out of breath.

"It's a nice little scar you've got there. You ought to see mine; fuckin' awful. I look like I've been attacked by Jack the bleeding Ripper."

"I haven't been out of bed yet to look at it." Erin could not help but smile at the woman's resilience.

"I'll get you a mirror out of my bag so you can see it."

From her forced supine position, Erin's eyes followed Irene as she hobbled over to her bedside cabinet. The older woman returned carrying a small hand-held makeup mirror.

"Take a look.  He's done a good job."

Erin was shocked when she looked in the mirror at the six inch angry red scar at the base of her neck. There was also a sore spot and a strange swelling on the right side of her bottom lip, and she was dismayed to notice that her complexion resembled that of a week-old corpse.

"Oh God; take it away." She handed back the mirror to its owner.

"You'll feel better tomorrow. There will be good days and bad days; tomorrow will be a good day."

"You don't say." She could feel the tears forming in the back of her eyes.

"I should know; I've been through it all before."
"I'll take your word for it then."

# CHAPTER 17

SHE FELT TOO wide awake to sleep. Every time she dozed off something jolted her awake again, making her feel sick and dizzy. She grimaced at Staff Nurse Imbeah, as the nurse took some observations and jotted down the findings.

"Still awake then Ms Mason?" Staff nurse clipped the notes back together and put her pen back in the top pocket of her tunic.

"I can't sleep."

"It's the reversing agent they give you. We often have patients that stay awake for three days. Others sleep for a week. Every patient processes the chemicals differently."

"Can I try and get up for a wee?"

"I'll bring the commode over for you. It'll be too far for you to walk to the toilet at the moment." Staff nurse disappeared through the curtains, pulling them together behind her.

Erin sat up slowly and swung her legs over the side of the bed. Her heart was racing and she felt as weak as a new-born baby. Slowly and shakily she stood up as the curtains parted again.

"Sit yourself down on the commode here, and I'll be along in a few minutes to help you back in bed."

She felt relieved to be able to jettison the bedpans. However, as she sat on the commode she had a strange feeling in her head, akin to an attack of pins and needles. She had never felt anything like it. The pins and needles inside her head increased, and she began to feel rather strange. When the staff nurse returned, Erin was in a state of mild panic.

"I don't feel right; there's pins and needles in my head." She felt woozy and disorientated.

"Back you get in bed and lay flat. You're having a little faint. Don't worry; you've probably got up too soon, and it's sent your blood pressure racing downwards."

Erin felt firm hands helping her back to bed. The staff nurse removed her pillows and used them instead to elevate her legs. As she lay flat on the bed she began to feel somewhat better, and breathed a sigh of relief as the pins and needles subsided.

"You'll be okay; lay like that for a while and then I'll come back and change the pillows round. Try and get some rest."

The nurse bustled off. Erin counted the flowers on the curtains and then counted them several more times, but infuriatingly each time she arrived at a different amount. The laboured breathing and loud snoring of the other slumbering patients irritated her immensely, and there was nothing else to do but constantly try to clear her throat and follow the hands of her watch around as they slowly moved towards 06:30. When the sun started to rise in the sky, footsteps approached her bed, and a pair of hands pulled back the florid curtains, revealing a plump, motherly woman of uncertain age. Erin sat up slowly to receive a cup of scalding anaemic-looking liquid.

"Cup of tea for you, love. I'm Elsie, one of the housekeepers."

"Thank you." She tried to cough and was grateful for the drink, which in her present parched state seemed like manna from heaven. She noticed with dismay that her voice was still absent.

"Breakfast is at half past eight when the hot-locks come round. Have I seen you somewhere before?" Elsie gave her a second glance.

"I work on Somerset ward."

"Oh yes; we had to deep-clean that one a couple of weeks' ago. That's where I must have seen you then. Lost your voice?"

"Something like that." She whispered, tried to sip the tea without choking, and wished that Elsie would go away.

"Hope you get better soon."

Erin watched as Elsie steered the tea trolley over to Irene, who was beginning to stir.

"Cup of tea, Irene." Elsie rattled a cup in its saucer.

"Fuck off."

Erin grinned as Irene emerged grumpily from sleep.

"I'll leave it on the side for you." Elsie, unsmiling, bashed the cup on the bedside cabinet and wheeled the trolley over towards the next patient.

Feeling less depressed than the day before, and greatly relieved that she had managed to sip the tea without choking, Erin acknowledged her new-found friend in the opposite bed.

"'Morning Irene." She cleared her throat yet again and risked a smile, hoping for an improvement on Elsie's response.

"Don't you start!  Have you got any fags?"

"Sorry, I don't smoke." Erin whispered as loudly as she could manage.

"I smoked me last one yesterday. I get a terrible strop on when I run out."

"Will you be having any visitors today? Perhaps they can bring some in for you."

"Only the old man. He wants me to give up, but I can't. I've been smoking since I was eleven." Irene sighed and rummaged in her bag in the hope of finding a stray cigarette.

"There's a shop down in the foyer. They'll sell some for sure."

"Is there? Cheers for that. I haven't been out of the ward yet. If the nurse asks where I've gone, tell her I've gone to the shop." Irene slurped the last of her tea and stood up, wrapping her dressing gown around her.

"Are you okay walking all that way?"

"I'm alright, it's all you other poor bastards I feel sorry for."

Erin bridled at the thought of anybody pitying her in her present predicament.

"I'm fine. I'm feeling much better today." She whispered and swallowed whatever was dripping down the back of her nose.

"You've got a bit more colour for sure. Anyway, I'm off; see ya later."

Erin lay back against the pillows and watched Irene's retreating back. The eight o'clock handover to the day shift began, and with the comfort of knowing that more members of staff were nearby, she decided to try and walk to the toilet.

It seemed like a massive undertaking. Shuffling along like an old woman, she hoped she would not feel faint again as she held on to the ends of the beds for support, feeling her heart pounding in her chest, and being aware of other patients' eyes upon her. She smiled to nobody in particular as she walked slowly to the sanctity of the toilet, hoping her behind was not hanging out of the back of her hospital gown. When at last she made it back to her bed she felt as though she had run a 26 mile marathon:

"Well done! Didn't feel faint this morning then?" A new nurse appeared at the side of her bed.

"No; not yet anyway. When can I have the nebuliser? I've got so much gunge in the back of my throat." She panted as she whispered out the words.

"After breakfast; you might feel a bit sick if you have it on an empty stomach. We'll help you have a wash; you can have your first thyroxine tablet, and then hopefully you might start to feel a bit better. It's a fast-acting kind, liothyronine, T3 for short, and you'll need to take three tablets every day. You'll have the slower-acting type, levothyroxine, T4 for short, a few weeks down the line."

"Why?"

"Well, you may need to come off it if you need radioiodine treatment. T3 doesn't stay in your bloodstream the way that T4 does, and your body needs to be totally clear of any thyroid hormone if you need radioiodine therapy."

T3;T4? It was all Greek to Erin. She shrugged her shoulders. *She didn't have cancer anyway; they'd told her at the start it was a multi-nodular goitre.*

# CHAPTER 18

AFTER A NEBULISER and a tentative wash at the sink, Erin felt she was back in the land of the living. She switched her mobile phone back on and immediately it pinged with three text messages.

*'How are U? We R having a gr8 time. Luv Kevin x'*

She smiled and knew almost by clairvoyance who had sent the other two.

*'Call me as soon as you are able to. Love Mum. X'*

*'Up and about yet?'* There was no name or kiss on this one, but then she thought ruefully that Chris had stopped kissing her a long time ago.

She silently thanked the inventor of texting, whilst tapping out messages to her family informing them that she was recovering, but did not want any visitors due to being only able to speak in a whisper.

*'Gr8. You can't shout at me anymore!'* Kieran's predictable reply caused her to chuckle.

*'I'm sure you'll soon get your voice back. I lost mine in 1958 for two months when I had laryngitis. We'll communicate by text then.'*

Erin pondered with interest if her loquacious mother might ever suffer a welcome relapse.

*'Get well soon.'* Chris' message was short and succinct.

"Got your voice back yet?" Irene, smelling faintly of cigarette smoke, hobbled over.

"No, but thankfully I know how to text." Erin smiled and whispered to her new-found friend.

"Tell 'em to all piss off. My old man knows not to come in until I tell him to." Irene cackled and coughed. "The doctors will be around soon. Hopefully we'll be able to go home soon." She held out a cigarette. "Want to start?"

"Thanks for the offer, but no. I've got enough gunge on my lungs as it is." Erin laughed and felt pleased at being able to give a slight but audible cough as she whispered.

"Fair enough. I'm off for another puff if the doctors don't turn up in a minute."

As though by magic the door to the bay opened to reveal the now familiar form of Mr Barker-Lomax. Erin sat up in bed and watched as the nurse accompanying the ward round pulled the curtains around her bed for privacy and handed her notes to the surgeon.

"Good morning Ms Mason. How are we feeling this morning?" The surgeon spoke to her neck as he peered over the top of his rimless spectacles.

"A lot better than yesterday. I've been up to the loo, and had a wash at the sink." She held her neck up for inspection as she whispered and tried to make eye contact.

"That's good.  Are you in any pain?"

"No, not really. My neck is stiff and I have no voice, but that's about it."

"It's early days yet." The surgeon wrote in the notes and clipped them back on the end of the bed. "You can go home tomorrow if you feel well enough. Continue to take three liothyronine tablets every day until you see me again in a fortnight. Nurse will make you an appointment, and we'll have the results of the biopsy available by then."

"Thank you, doctor."

In the blink of an eye he had gone on to the next patient, leaving Erin feeling as though she had become a soulless neck on legs. The curtains were pulled back slightly, revealing a young and rather handsome looking man standing before her with floppy brown hair, who was wearing a green tunic coat and black trousers:

"Hello; I'm Jason, the physiotherapist. I've come to show you how to do some breathing exercises to help clear your throat." He smiled as he drew the curtains again and unclipped the notes from the bedrail. "Have they started your nebulisers yet?"

"Yes, I'm to have one after every meal. I've had the breakfast one already." Erin wished she could be left alone to sleep for a week.

"Let's have you out of bed and sitting in your chair, and then we can start."

Jason's voice was unusually bright and cheerful. Erin hauled herself out of bed and waited as the physiotherapist brought a visitor's chair over to the bedside and sat himself down opposite her.

"We're going to take some big breaths; in and out, and in and out."

Erin could not help but notice how good-looking he was. As he breathed in and out with her, she had to stifle a giggle.

"Take several of these big breaths a few times every day to help clear your body of the anaesthetic gases, and instead of trying to cough, which I know you can't, just use the muscles at the back of your throat to clear the phlegm." A guttural sound emitted from the region of his Adam's apple.

Erin could almost feel the other patients' mirth on the other side of the closed curtains. However, as she harrumphed and hacked along with Jason like two Arabs in a bazaar, she had to reluctantly admit that the exercises were in fact beneficial.

"Here's your TTO's. You'll be free to go home tomorrow evening after your last nebuliser."

Erin smiled at the nurse as she took a paper bag from her containing a two week supply of precious T3, and felt surprised to be let home so soon:

"Is that right I have to take them on an empty stomach?"

"Not necessarily; the longer-acting ones maybe. Your GP will prescribe more when you give him the discharge letter." The nurse handed her an accompanying envelope, and unclipped the notes to write on an empty page.

"Thank you. I'll text my mother to pick me up, but could you phone her as well please? I can't talk much."

"Of course. I'll do that now for you."

The nurse disappeared, leaving Erin clutching the bag of tablets. She held them up to Irene in a clenched fist, and with a huge grin on her face.

"Well done. Hope it all goes well for you. You sure you don't want a fag?" Irene held up a packet of cigarettes and opened the top. Erin shook her head:

"Cheers Irene. Hope everything works out okay for you as well. Looks like I'm going home tomorrow." She smiled, but wondered which one of them would die first.

# CHAPTER 19

ALAN WAS AWARE of various unfamiliar sounds as he lay flat on his back and drifted in and out of consciousness. Trolleys rattled, high-pitched female voices laughed and chattered, and from somewhere along the corridor he could hear two people hacking loudly and clearing the backs of their throats.

"Aha! Back in the land of the living! We've brought you from Recovery, and you're now back on the ward." A disembodied voice prattled in his left ear.

Alan opened his eyes to the sight of a smiling nurse, wracked his woolly brain, and tried to remember being in Recovery, but for the life of him he could not.

"Water; please can I have some water." He ran his tongue around his mouth, which felt like the bottom of a parrot's cage. His neck felt stiff and unyielding.

"Just sips for now." The nurse stood over him with a cup and a straw.

Lifting himself up slightly to suck on the straw, Alan felt the room sway around. He took a small sip, and coughed.

"I'm choking!" He tried not to show any panic.

"Your throat will soon get used to the new norm. You'll be fine; don't worry."

Alan was not convinced. Coughing and spluttering, he laid back on the pillows and swallowed repeatedly.

"Your voice sounds good. Some people aren't so lucky." The nurse smiled as she placed the cup on Alan's bedside cabinet.

Alan did not feel particularly lucky. He swallowed again and took several deep breaths to calm himself. He reached a hand up to touch the front of his neck.

"Don't touch the scar, Mr Beaumont. It's a nice little scar; when it heals you'll hardly notice it. You'll be able to eat after a few hours when the anaesthetic wears off; lay back and relax for now."

The nurse wandered off, leaving Alan to his own devices. He closed his eyes, trying to shut out the sounds of the staff going about their daily routines. He realised that he must have drifted off to sleep again, as when he awoke some time later a porter was collecting empty dinner plates, and he had a terrible raging hunger and thirst. The straw was still in the cup of water where the nurse had left it previously, but somebody else had also been by to leave a plate of sandwiches wrapped in clingfilm next to the cup. Alan took some grateful sips of water and a bite or two of one of the sandwiches, and then he slumped back on his pillows again and stared at the ceiling.

*How could he have had cancer in his body and not known about it? How long had the cancer been there? Had it spread? If so, was he going to die? Would he ever be able to move his neck again? How could he stop Tilly coming in to see him like this?*

"Alright, mate?"

Alan's thoughts were interrupted by a voice close to him. He lowered his gaze to see the figure of a sturdily-built balding man somewhere in his mid-sixties standing in a pair of blue stripy pyjamas at the end of his bed.

"Don't know yet." He wished the man would go away.

"I've just had me Chalfonts done; can't sit down now. Fuckin' awful pain."

"I bet." Alan suddenly wanted to smile at the Cockney slang, but decided against it.

"Name's Bill. If the fucker who twisted that knife up my arse comes in here I'm gonna slap him one."

"Sorry to laugh, but I can't help it." In the depths of his misery, Alan could not stop a bubbling mirth rising in his throat.

"S'all right mate; everyone laughs at Chalfonts don't they? I have to tell you though, it's bloody miserable when you've got them."

"I know. I remember my old man was like a bear with a sore head when he had his done." Alan sat up in bed and rubbed his eyes.

"Sore arse more like. You look a bit rough, mate; what they done to you?" Bill adjusted the back of his pyjama bottoms until they felt more comfortable.

"I've had my thyroid out." He hesitated, but could not bring himself to declare the reason why. He still felt as though it could all be a bad dream from which he might awaken any time soon.

"Sounds nasty; I think I'll stick to me Chalfonts." Bill gave him a cheery wave and waddled back to his bed opposite. Alan likened the man's gait to John Wayne after a week in the saddle.

"We're back in the land of the living are we, Mr Beaumont?"

Alan wished everybody would leave him alone. A new nurse had appeared whom he had not seen before, and with some irritation he noticed Bill across the other side of the bay watching and listening to every word of the conversation.

"I'm okay, I think. I need a wee though."

"I'll bring you a bottle; you'll be able to get up tomorrow, and maybe even go home if Mr Barker-Lomax says you're fit for discharge. I'll check your pulse and blood pressure in a minute. Oh, and your daughter rang this morning; I told her you were back on the ward and sleeping."

"Thanks; I don't really want any visitors today." "She's already been in tonight, but you were out cold." With some surprise Alan looked at his watch; it was seven o'clock in the evening. He had lost almost a whole day.

"This is your first thyroxine tablet. You'll need to take one every morning, one every lunchtime, and one every evening until you see Mr Barker-Lomax again for your follow up appointment. He'll tell you where to go from there. We'll give you enough tablets for a week, but then you'll have to give your GP our discharge letter to obtain a regular supply." The nurse held out a small plastic container.

Alan looked at the tiny white tablet in the pot and shrugged his shoulders:

"What good will that do?"

"You'll be surprised, Mr Beaumont. Those little pills are going to keep you alive for the rest of your natural." The nurse gave a chuckle and reached out her hand again to take back the empty pill box.

# CHAPTER 20

"ONCE I HAD a stiff neck for three weeks. I couldn't turn my head at all. Never known pain like it."

*Oh no, here we go again…..*

Erin fastened her seat belt, closed her eyes, and tried to use subtle body language to impart the fact that she did not want to use her weakened voice. However, she soon realised that now her mother had a captive audience, she was not to be dissuaded from re-gorging virtually every ache and pain that she had ever suffered from.

"Dad had to wash my hair. I thought my neck would get stuck like it, but that was nothing compared to my fibrositis a year later."

The effect of the anaesthetic must have still been lingering in her body, because when Erin woke up with a jolt a while later, her mother had brought the car to a standstill at the traffic lights, but was still talking. Trying to turn her head towards the window to hide a grin as best she could, Erin likened her mother's verbosity to a machine gun.

*She has enough jaw for ten rows of teeth………*

When the car's engine eventually stopped, Erin thanked the Lord above and opened the passenger door.

"I've brought all my night stuff. I'll sleep in one of the boys' beds. Someone's got to look after you."

Erin whispered to her mother as she watched her grabbing luggage from the back seat, together with her own holdall.

"Really; I'm fine. You don't have to." She felt anything *but* fine. However, she relished an empty house, peace and quiet, and not having to talk to anybody at all.

"Rubbish; look at the state of you. You look like you've seen a ghost. There's no way I'm leaving you here own your own tonight."

Feeling slightly relieved that there would be somebody in the house after all, Erin walked slowly with leaden feet to her front door and turned the key in the lock. A faint smell of boys assailed her nostrils and made her ache for her sons' cheerful company.

"Just for tonight then; I'll be okay after tomorrow."

She felt as though she'd been hit with a ten-ton truck, and could not wait to get into bed; even putting up no resistance as her mother fussed and fretted over her. Erin barely had the strength to undress. She cleaned her teeth, took her third T3 tablet of the day, and laid her head on her comfortable pillow, glad to be home amongst familiar surroundings.

"I'm just next door.  Shout if you need me."

"I can't shout, Mum. I've got no voice, remember?" Erin kept her eyes closed and whispered with a hint of irritation.

"Oh yes, I forgot. Did I tell you about the time I lost my voice?"

"Probably."

"I'll put the telly on then and make a nice cup of tea."

"Okay."

When she woke up she could hear the birds singing, and the cup of tea her mother had brought in the night before still sat untouched on her bedside table. Erin yawned and sat up slowly. She could hear her mother rattling cups and plates in the kitchen, and Radio Four could be heard blaring out through the thin walls. *She hated Radio Four.*

Her heart was pounding as stood shakily and eased her feet into her slippers. She took a T3 tablet from the packet by her bed, and took a sip of water from a glass next to the cold cup of tea. Taking it slowly, she walked towards the kitchen.

"Can you turn the volume down please?" She whispered and pointed towards the radio standing next to her mother.

"I like Radio four." Cynthia shouted over the prattle of the announcer.

Her mother even made a cup of tea noisily. Erin flinched at the intrusion into her privacy, and sunk down onto a nearby kitchen chair.

"Cup of tea, love?" Cynthia added two teaspoons of sugar to both mugs and poured boiling water into a teapot.

"I don't have sugar." Erin whispered, as she upended the mug back into the sugar bowl.

"You used to."

"Yeah; when I was ten and had no choice. Have you got the heat on?" She felt hot and shaky, and her heart was pounding away.

"I turned the thermostat up; I was a bit cold."

"You're always cold. I'm boiling." She stood up again, walked to the thermostat, and turned it down. She noticed with horror that her mother had turned it up to 28 degrees Centigrade.

"Aw; it was just warming up in here." Cynthia *tutted* and poured out some tea. "Here you are; would you like some bacon and eggs?"

"No thanks, Mum. I think I'll just have some cereal." Erin whispered with some effort.

"I used the last of the milk on mine an hour ago. The milkman hasn't been yet."

"Doesn't matter. I'll drink this and have a wash, but I think I'll need some help with my hair; every time I move my neck it pulls on the stitches." She panted with the effort of whispering, and fingered the hard line at the base of her neck.

"I can wash your hair with the shower attachment if you kneel over the bath."

"Okay, but I mustn't get my stitches wet."

She felt five years old again as she let her mother shampoo and rinse her hair. It did make her feel a bit better though, but by the time she had managed to get herself washed and dressed she was ready to sit down again; her heart was pounding and she felt exhausted.

"That operation's really taken it out of you, I can tell." Cynthia looked with some concern at her daughter.

"I'll be alright in a few days. It's just that my heart's pounding and pounding." Erin whispered and sweated, and wanted to cry for no real reason.

"I'll phone the ward for you. They said you could phone them if you had any questions."

"Thanks, Mum. Tell them my heart won't stop racing." She sighed and laid down on the settee. *Something wasn't right!*

"I had all that in my change; palpitations for years and night sweats you wouldn't believe. Do you know, I had to have showers in the middle of the night! Are you going through the change yet?"

"No.  I've got that joy to come."

She could hear her mother as she spoke on the kitchen telephone to the ward. She wondered if Irene was still an in-patient and could hear the conversation at the other end.

"They paged your surgeon, and he said to take two tablets instead of three; one in the morning and one in the evening. I still say it might be the change though." Cynthia stood in the lounge doorway, one hand on her hip.

"Cheers, Mum.  I'll try two tablets instead."

# CHAPTER 21

"CALL ME IF you need me; I'm only twenty minutes' away."
Cynthia picked up her holdall and opened the front door.

"I'm feeling better now on the two tablets. Thanks for cooking and cleaning for me; I'll give you a ring when I've seen the surgeon." Erin whispered and smiled.

"You do that. I can stay longer if you like; there's nothing I need to get home for."

Erin gave her mother a hug.

"I'm okay; really." *You need to get home before I lose my mind!*

"Well, give me a ring; I'm always on the other end of the phone."

"I will."

With a sigh of relief Erin closed the front door behind her mother and leaned briefly against the frosted glass. She felt exhausted with continually trying to speak, and relished the peace and quiet of her empty house. With everybody gone she could potter around doing just what she liked, and if she wanted to lie in bed all day, then that was exactly what she would do.

After a fortnight when her appointment had come around with the surgeon, Erin was feeling more like her normal self. Most of her strength had been regained, she had been able to walk to the local shops, her wound had healed nicely, and it was a treat to be able to stand in the shower again. She had started to miss her boys, and looked forward to their daily telephone calls, even though she still could only whisper. As she left home on a pleasant late-summer morning to see the surgeon, the only issue she had was the non-return of her voice.

"Ms Mason! Do come in! How are you today?"

Erin shook Mr Barker-Lomax's hand and felt relieved that he was smiling.

"I'm feeling a lot better now, thanks, but I've still not got much of a voice." She returned his smile as she sat down.

"That will improve over time. Your wound seems to be healing well though." He peered over the top of his glasses at her neck.

"Oh, good." Erin wondered how long her voice would take to improve, but decided not to ask any further questions.

The surgeon shuffled some papers and adjusted his glasses. Erin looked hopefully in his direction.

"Ms Mason; er……we have the results back from the biopsy of your thyroid gland. I'm afraid I have to tell you that the thyroid gland *was* cancerous, as I had suspected."

Erin felt her good humour slide away, to be replaced with a sinking feeling in the pit of her stomach. She held on tightly to the arms of the chair.

"However, you have the most common type which is often easily treatable; papillary thyroid cancer. Unfortunately though, histology also tells us that the cancer is at stage four, which means it has spread outside the thyroid to the surrounding lymph nodes, which when removed and biopsied were also cancerous….." The surgeon coughed, adjusted his glasses again, and shuffled his papers a bit more.

Erin stared at him uncomprehendingly; she could not believe the words she had just heard the surgeon say so clearly. Her brain raced: *How could she have advanced cancer? She had felt so well! Surely people with advanced cancer would be at death's door?*

"How long have I got left?" Her eyes filled with tears, and her whole life flashed before her as she whispered in a trembling voice.

"Papillary thyroid cancer usually responds well to radioactive iodine treatment. You will need to have possibly three of these treatments, and for this I will need to refer you to an oncologist here. I will also refer you to the Ear, Nose and Throat department who can help with your voice. Because the cancer was er…advanced and removal of the thyroid gland was difficult, the vocal cords suffered manipulation and bruising in the process. Your voice will return to normal in time."

Erin watched the surgeon writing in her notes as though in a trance.

"What do I need to do now?" Her voice came out teary, cracked and broken.

"Appointments will be sent to you from the oncologist and from the ear, nose and throat department. Try not to worry; our oncologist is very good at treating thyroid cancer. He'll take great care of you." The surgeon attempted a smile as he closed his files.

Erin realised she was being dismissed, and stumbled out of the consultant's room; her head spinning with a myriad of questions: *How on earth could she have advanced cancer and still be walking about? Would she live to see her boys grown up? How could she tell them she might die? Should she cancel next year's holiday? Who would give her travel insurance now? What would her ward manager and friends at work say when they found out? And the scariest one of all....how could she tell her mother without sending her into an out-of-control panic attack?*

By the time she had driven home, Erin was certain of one thing; she was definitely not going to tell her mother anything. *What Cynthia didn't know, Cynthia wouldn't grieve over.*

# CHAPTER 22

"I'VE TOLD THE boys. Kevin wants to come home and look after you."

"I'm fine honestly. It's best he stays with you. I'm finding it difficult to talk at the moment." Erin panted for breath as she whispered into the phone. "I can look after myself. I've just got to wait for an appointment now to see the oncologist. I'm getting sick pay; the GP has signed me off for another month. But hopefully my voice might have returned by then."

"We're coming round for a visit later on anyway. I want to make sure you're okay."

There was obvious concern in her ex-husband's voice, and Erin replaced the receiver with a surprised look on her face. Chris had never been one to show his feelings too much; his overly-macho exterior did not usually permit any soft side he might possess to intrude, and every day she could see Kieran becoming more and more like his father. She knew she had always felt closer to Kevin, who unlike his twin, from an early age had picked up a double dose of the compassion and empathy gene that had seemingly bypassed his brother.

*Should she cook them something? Marie would probably have made them dinner anyway.* Erin checked her cupboards for enough tea, coffee and biscuits, and decided to make herself look as good as possible for the visit; she hated the thought of anybody feeling sorry for her. She took a long bath and washed her hair, applied some make-up and a touch of foundation over the scar, and put on a clean pair of jeans and a pretty top. She took great care blow-drying her hair into a sleek red bob, and was admiring herself in the hall mirror as the doorbell rang a couple of hours' later.

"Hi Mum!" Kevin was first through the door and flung his arms around her. "You look great!"

"Thanks, love." Erin whispered and wanted to cry as she hugged him. "It's so good to see you!"

"I can beat Kevin at 'The Walking Dead!'" Kieran kissed her briefly on the cheek.

"Sounds grim! That's what I feel like at the moment!" Erin smiled and ruffled his hair.

"No; you're fine. As Kevin says, you look great." Chris stepped over the threshold and smiled awkwardly at her.

"Thanks; I'm feeling a lot better now, although it doesn't sound like it." Erin closed the front door and followed behind them into the lounge. For a split second it seemed like old times again, although in the past she knew that Chris would have kissed and cuddled her just as much as Kevin had. She looked at the back of the twins' red heads and Chris' curly brown one, and wanted to reach out and hold onto the moment forever.

"Who wants a drink? Chris; can I get you some tea or coffee?"

"Tea please."

"Boys?"

"We're okay. We just have to go to our room and sort out some more games." Kevin and Kieran answered as one, and raced each other up the stairs.

She saw Chris make himself comfortable in his old armchair, and smiled at him.

"I'll put the kettle on then. The boys seem as energetic as ever."

"Yeah; they're a bit of a handful for Marie. She's only been used to Freddie all day."

"It won't be forever; perhaps just another week or so."

"It's okay; we'll keep them until they go back to college. It'll give your voice a chance to recover." Chris yawned and stretched out in the chair. "It feels funny sitting here again."

"It's been a long time since you sat there." Erin stood in the doorway and smiled.

"Yeah, a lot of water's gone under the bridge, but it's good that we've been able to remain friends." Chris returned the smile.

When she returned with two cups of tea and a plate of biscuits, she saw that her ex-husband's eyes were closed.

"Wakey wakey, tea's up. Marie'll be wondering where you've gone."

"No, she's fine; she trusts me. She wanted me to help you."

A *frisson* of jealousy shot through Erin's body as she sat in the armchair opposite him.

"Help yourself to biscuits before the locusts appear. Have you noticed your food bill increase yet?" She quickly masked the envy, laughed, and dipped a biscuit in her tea.

"Have I heck; it's like feeding the five thousand. I'm sure *I* was never as hungry as those two when I was their age." Chris shook his head and picked up a biscuit.

"I think they have eating contests to see who can demolish the most food." Erin looked up as thumps could be heard in one of the bedrooms. "They're play fighting now. Kevin will come off worst; he always does."

"Can I do anything for you before I go home?" Chris tipped up his cup and drunk half the tea in one go.

"I don't think so. I'm waiting for an appointment with the oncologist now, and then we'll see what happens next."

"Don't forget I'm on the other end of the phone. You don't have to suffer alone."

"Thanks, Chris." She smiled gratefully.

A virtual herd of elephants made their way down the stairs.

"You never said there were biscuits!" Kieran picked up three. "There's none left for you, turd boy." He kicked his brother and flopped down on the settee.

"Any more in the packet, Mum?" Kevin's dismay at the sight of the empty plate was almost palpable.

"Yes; you know where they are." Erin whispered. "Help yourself."

"When can we come home?" Kevin stopped in the doorway on his way to the kitchen.

"Dad said you can stay with him until you go back to college. It'll give my voice time to recover, then I'll be able to shout at the pair of you all day long."

"So what's new?" Kieran volunteered with his mouth full of biscuit.

"Cheers, Kieran." Erin giggled.

"Are you going to be alright, Mum?" Kevin returned with the packet of biscuits and perched on the armchair next to Erin.

"I've probably got to have some radiation treatment, but the doctor says I'll be okay in the long run." She gave her son a quick squeeze.

"Good news then I suppose?" Chris placed his cup down on the coffee table.

"In a way; they say it's a *'good'* cancer, whatever that means." Erin shrugged her shoulders.

"Well, we're all rooting for you, you know that. Come on bombheads; say goodbye to your mother and then we'll leave her in peace and go back." Chris yawned again and stood up.

Erin laughed as Kevin almost threw himself on her.

"Bye Mum; love you."

"Love you too; see you soon." She kissed the top of his head.

"Bye Mum; we'll come back every week to haunt you." Kieran gave her a kiss.

"See you in a few days I expect, or whenever you want to cycle round. I'll be here, sunning myself in the garden." She stood between her sons and put her arms around their waists.

"We're taller than you now." Kevin looked down on her and smiled.

"I know; I'll have to stop feeding you two I think."

"That's it then; we're staying with Dad and Marie." Kieran chuckled.

She realised she had missed the boys' banter, and was quite sad to see them depart. Chris stood awkwardly in front of her, not knowing what to do.

"Bye Chris; thanks for coming round." She moved towards the front door and opened it, wanting to spare him any embarrassment.

"Bye Erin; look after yourself." He walked past her and out into the garden.

"I will; I'll be as good as new in no time."

"See ya." He waved and opened the car's central locking. "In you get boys."

She was still smiling as she watched the car stop at the end of the road before turning right. Kevin's arm was still waving out of the window.

# CHAPTER 23

"MR BEAUMONT!" HOW has it been for you these past couple of weeks?" Mr Barker-Lomax stood up from his chair, held out his hand, and peered over the top of his spectacles.

Alan gave his firmest handshake, and wondered if he ought to mention the fact that he was already working part-time back at the garage:

"Not too bad actually; the scar's healing okay. At last I've had an excuse why I couldn't wash or shave." He chuckled, took a seat, and decided against imparting too much information.

"Well let's see......." The surgeon pushed his glasses up to the bridge of his nose, sat down, and looked at his computer screen. "We have your results back, and unfortunately I'm afraid that the biopsy has confirmed our suspicions of papillary thyroid cancer. Your cancer is at stage three, which means it has spread just slightly outside of the thyroid. Fortunately your voice seems unaffected. I suggest treatment with radioactive iodine to kill any remaining cancer cells in the thyroid bed and surrounding tissue. This treatment will also mop up any rogue thyroid cancer cells circulating in the body."

Alan's heart sank as the last remaining vestige of hope died.

"Is there no alternative?"

"It's best that you undergo treatment so that there are no thyroid cancer cells left to travel in the bloodstream and metastasise in other areas. If you agree I will refer you to our oncologist Stephen Ingram, who will add you to his waiting list." The surgeon turned around in his seat and looked at Alan hopefully.

"What are the side-effects of the radiation?" Alan did not like the sound of it.

"Well, it may cause temporary nausea and vomiting. You might be prone to colds and 'flu for a while. Your salivary glands might be rather swollen and sore for some time, and there is a small chance of contracting a different type of cancer possibly at some point in the future. You may notice a difference in taste, you may have a sore throat, and you may have a dry mouth or eye problems. In men sometimes it causes a low sperm count. However, you may have none of these symptoms at all." The surgeon smiled as he waited for an answer.

Alan liked the sound of it even less.

"A low sperm count is the least of my problems. Which other type of cancer could it cause then?"

"It may never cause any other type of cancer at all, but I have to mention that you may be at risk of leukaemia in years to come."

"I'm between the devil and the deep blue sea then, aren't I? I'm damned if I do, and damned if I don't." Alan sighed and had not the foggiest idea of how to proceed.

"You have more of a fighting chance if you undergo the treatment." Mr Barker-Lomax nodded to emphasise his statement.

Alan had tried to fight the outcome, but it was no use. His shoulders slumped as he took in the inevitability of the news.

"Okay then doc; sign me up. Whatever; I'll do it."

"A wise decision Mr Beaumont. You will be hearing from Dr Ingram in the very near future." Mr Barker-Lomax swung around to his desk and wrote something on a pad of paper, before standing up and extending his hand. "Keep taking your thyroxine tablets; do you feel well on the three times daily dose?"

"No problems in that direction."

"Energy levels okay?"

"Yeah; fine. I'm back at work now."

"Wonderful! I'm sure the treatment will be entirely successful for you. You will have to stop taking the tablets for a fortnight before the treatment, so you will feel tired as the date for the radiation approaches. It's best you stop work for that fortnight and also for another fortnight afterwards to let the thyroxine levels come back up. You'll need to take it easy for a bit."

"Cheers." With a low sigh of resignation, Alan stood up, gave the surgeon another firm handshake, and walked back to his car; hating the thought of having to be dependent on Matthew's goodwill yet again.

"You're back early!" Matthew raised his head up from the bonnet of a black Honda Jazz, and flashed an irritating smile showing even white teeth.

"Yeah; I've got to have more treatment. It's cancer, just as they thought in the first place." Alan felt somehow relieved to be able to share his burden.

Matthew let a spanner crash to the floor, a look of concern appearing on his face.

"Christ! Have you told Tilly it's confirmed?"

"Not yet. I haven't been home."

"What are they going to do about it then?"

"I've got to have some radiation treatment. You'll have to carry on here again on your own for quite a few weeks I think."

"No probs.  I'll do whatever I can to help."

Alan was aware of a faint shiver of jealousy snaking through his body at the sight of the fit, young man standing before him. He felt old, washed-up, and so very, very ANGRY!

Within a month or so he was holding an unfamiliar appointment card in his hand as he sat facing another young, hale and hearty individual; his new oncologist Doctor Stephen Ingram.

# CHAPTER 24

"HELLO, MRS MASON, do come in!" The oncologist waved her towards a desk and two chairs.

"Nice to meet you Doctor Ingram, but it's Ms if you don't mind." Erin smiled at the personable thirty-something doctor, and seated herself on the chair nearest his desk.

"Of course, Ms Mason; Mr Barker-Lomax sent you along to me. How much has he told you about your condition?" Dr Ingram riffled through his notes and ran a hand through his unruly blond hair.

"He's said that I have papillary thyroid cancer that has spread outside the thyroid gland." Erin could still hardly believe it herself as she uttered the words.

Dr Ingram nodded.

"Yes; that's right. You'll need some radioiodine therapy in our MacMillan Unit. I'll just feel around your neck if I may, and if you are in agreement I'll book you in to the Radioiodine Suite. There's a bit of a waiting list, but you'll be called in for treatment in about a month's time."

"Yes; if I need treatment, then I'll have to have it I suppose. I've got two boys to bring up." Erin sighed and watched as the oncologist filled out a consent form, before bidding her to sit on the examination chair in the middle of the room.

The doctor's fingers were cold on her neck. Erin tried not to shudder at the unpleasant sensation of somebody touching her scar and pressing their fingers down at the top end of her sternum.

"Two weeks before your stay in the Radioiodine Suite, you will need to stop taking your T3 tablets. This is to make any remaining thyroid cells hungry for the iodine they need to function properly. You will also need to eat a low iodine diet in that two weeks; therefore no fish, no dairy products, and no food containing red colouring, for instance Maraschino cherries. This is so any thyroid cancer cells left in your body will gobble up the radioactive iodine you will be given, and be killed." Doctor Ingram washed his hands and sat down again.

"Wow; as easy as that?" Erin looked at the doctor incredulously.

"Well; there is a down side. You will feel quite tired when you stop taking the T3 tablets." Dr Ingram's brown eyes bored into hers. "You won't be able to work, and will possibly just want to sleep a lot of the time."

"Oh; there's always a snag isn't there?" Erin forced a grin and gave another sigh. "I've been signed off work anyway."

"However; if you need a second dose of radioactive iodine you will be able to have thyrogen injections instead and not come off the T3, but for the first dose it is best that the T3 tablets are stopped."

"I see; how will I know when to stop taking them?"

"We'll send you an appointment in the post for your first dose, so stop taking the tablets a fortnight before you come in. You'll need to stay in for about three days until radiation levels have subsided in your body."

"Will I be on a ward then?" Erin wracked her brain, but could not remember ever seeing a Radioiodine Suite on the MacMillan Unit.

"No; we have two lead-lined rooms hidden away for radioiodine patients. Each patient has their own room and shower, but you will not be allowed out of the suite until the physicist has confirmed your radiation levels have decreased to an acceptable level. However, you are allowed to converse with the patient in the next room if you so wish, so you are not totally on your own."

"Well, that's some comfort anyway." Erin shrugged her shoulders.

The chair scraped slightly on the floor as the doctor moved it backwards to stand up.

"That's all for now Ms Mason; more instructions about your treatment will be sent to you with your appointment. Carry on with your T3's for now, and we'll see you in the Radioiodine suite soon. Do you have any questions?" He held out his arm.

Erin shook his hand and nodded.

"How am I given the radiation?"

"You drink it. The physicist will bring it to the suite in a special lead-lined container."

"Oh God; that sounds grim." Erin exhaled and silently wished she had said nothing.

"It's perfectly safe. Radioactive iodine will only attack any remaining thyroid tissue."

"Have I got a choice as to whether to take it or not?"

"Of course; but it's best to go through with it to kill off any remaining thyroid cancer cells before they spread anywhere else in your body."

"When you put it like that, then I suppose I can't do anything *but* agree with you."

"Well, it'll be better for you in the long term if you do." Doctor Ingram nodded and smiled.

As Erin left the consulting room, she wondered what on earth she had let herself in for.

# CHAPTER 25

"MR BEAUMONT; PLEASED to meet you!" Dr Ingram ran a hand through his tousled blond locks with his left hand, and held out his right.

"How's it going doc?" Alan pumped the outstretched hand and wondered if every bastard in the world was younger and fitter than he was.

"Please take a seat. Mr Barker-Lomax sent through your referral." Dr Ingram smiled and indicated towards an empty chair next to his desk.

"Yeah; he said he would." Alan sat down and hoped he'd made a good show of hiding his nervousness.

There was a silence while the oncologist read through his notes. Alan took a minute to glance around the room at the examination couch, the sink with its elongated handles on the taps, the anatomical posters on the walls, the long bench with various medical packs stacked in orderly bundles on it, and finally at the infuriatingly young and good-looking doctor holding his patients' lives in the palms of his unlined hands.

"How much do you know about your condition?"

Alan was conscious of the oncologist peering at the scar on his neck as he spoke.

"Enough; the surgeon told me I've got to have radiation treatment. He told me all about the side-effects, but I'm wondering about one of them." Alan shifted on his seat and looked at the floor in embarrassment.

"Yes?" The oncologist looked at Alan hopefully.

"Well, when he said the sperm count goes down, I was wondering also about well…..you know…the old chap." Alan felt as though he wanted to shrink into the carpet.

"You're worried that you won't be able to have an erection after the treatment?" The oncologist's face was deadpan.

"Yeah; something like that."

"Let me assure you Mr Beaumont, if you have no trouble in that department now, you'll find there'll be no problems with it afterwards either. It might knock your salivary glands and immune system out for a while, but that's all." Doctor Ingram's face softened and smiled.

"Well, that's a relief then!" Alan tried to grin in return, but the effort more resembled a grimace.

"Are you happy to sign a consent form? We'll be able to call you in quite soon. We have two radioiodine rooms in our MacMillan Unit. The physicist will administer the radiation in the form of a drink, and you'll need to keep showering to bring your radiation levels down. Each room has its own shower of course, and although you can't step out of the suite, you'll be able to talk freely with the person having treatment in the other room if they so wish."

"I see. What will happen about receiving meals then?" Alan's imagination started to take flight.

"Meals and drinks will be served through a hatch. When the porters deliver food to the other patients on the ward, they'll put yours in the hatch, close their end, and then ring a bell to let you know it's there. You take your meal out of the hatch and close your side of it. Wash up all crockery afterwards and leave it in your room. You'll be able to order your meals in advance for the three days you'll be in the suite, and you can give some money to the housekeepers before your treatment and they can put a newspaper through the hatch every day. It's just important that nothing goes out of the suite until the physicist gives the okay." The oncologist looked keenly at his patient to gauge the response.

"Wow; I'll be really holed up then, won't I? No visitors I take it?" Alan tried to hide the disappointment in his voice.

"Visitors can be allowed, but for only twenty minutes at a time. They will have to wear protective clothing and stand as far away from you as possible. Obviously no pregnant women or young persons."

"No; I won't want anybody to visit. It's not worth taking the risk." Alan sighed and exhaled slowly.

"Exactly. On a lighter note though, you'll have a free telephone in your room to make as many calls as you wish."

"Great; I'll be phoning my brother in New Zealand then." Alan scanned the doctor's face for a reaction.

"Within reason, Mr Beaumont. UK calls only are permitted."

"Just joking doc; I haven't got a brother. I've got a sister in Newcastle though."

"Calls to Newcastle are allowed, or is it coals to Newcastle? Well, Mr Beaumont; I'll just examine your neck, and then you'll be free to go after you've signed the consent form. Instructions about stopping your thyroxine tablets beforehand will be sent to you, along with the low iodine diet you will have to follow, and the possible symptoms of hypothyroidism."

"Eh?"

"Low thyroxine levels in the body. You'll probably feel tired and fairly unwell once you stop your tablets."

"Oh no doc; I'm a fit bloke. I'll be as right as rain." Alan hated people who constantly whinged about how tired they were all the time.

"Fair enough. I look forward to seeing you in the Radioiodine suite. There's a few patients in front of you on the list, but it won't be too long a wait. I'll be popping my head around the door briefly on the second day of your stay there, but obviously not on the first day as the radiation levels in your room will be too high."

"Oh, so I will see somebody while I'm there then?" Alan's voice took on a more hopeful sound.

"Of course. Don't forget you can speak to the other person also having treatment in the next room, if your sister in Newcastle's not answering the phone." A smile played around the oncologist's lips.

"Oh yeah; I'd forgotten about that." Alan wondered who the other person would be, and if they would tell him to piss off if he ambled along and knocked on their door.

# CHAPTER 26

ERIN LISTENED AS Kevin read out the instructions once more, to try and get her head around the requirements.

"No dairy products; no fish; no seaweed such as in Chinese food, and no food containing red colorants. Date of treatment is Monday nineteenth of October. To stop all thyroxine supplementation on Monday the fifth October until after completion of radioiodine treatment. Mum; we'll have to have a well good slap up meal on the Sunday before!" Kevin grinned and slid the piece of paper along the table.

"You bet we will. Shall we push the boat out and book a table at The Regency hotel? I'm still getting sick pay, and I say sod the expense!" Erin whispered as loudly as she could.

"Yeah; it'll beat Marie's cooking. Kieran'll be up for it I know."

Erin looked fondly over at her son.

"How are you getting on over there? Sorry about you having had to stay with Dad all this time."

"It's okay, but I'm definitely coming home to look after you before you have the treatment. I can make you some food before I go to college, and then cook you something in the evening if you're too tired to do anything."

Her eyes filled with tears at the thought of it.

"Kevin, you mustn't ………"

"I don't care. I know you and Nan don't get on. I know she'll have to drive you to the hospital, but I'll be around until then. Nan will only want you to talk to her all the time, and it'll make you feel worse."

"Sorry for the tears; I've got such a lovely boy." Erin wiped her eyes. "Will Kieran stay with Dad then?"

"Yeah; he'll only wind me up." He walked over to her where she sat at the kitchen table, and gave her a cuddle. "I'm coming back here after the Regency dinner. You won't get rid of me, no matter how hard you try."

"I don't want to get rid of you." Her tears flowed freely again.

"Love you Mum."

"Love you too Kevin. Now off you go and keep an eye on that brother of yours."

After he had cycled back to his father, Erin decided to make a list of food she liked that would be allowed, and that Kevin would know how to cook. She decided on beef burgers and chips (no tomato sauce), variations on a chicken theme and vegetables, sausages and jacket potatoes, and turkey steaks and savoury rice. She would go all out at the Regency and order her favourite salmon or trout, with a mountain of veggies and cheesy sauce. The boys would probably plump for fillet steaks, but she was determined to let them have whatever they wanted. *To hell with the cost!!*

It was Chris who was to give her the biggest surprise of all; on the Sunday morning of the 4th of October he delivered both boys in time for her to drive them to the Regency, but as the twins went towards her car he hung back as she locked the front door.

"Here; this is for the dinner." He pushed three crisp twenty pound notes into her hand. "Hope the treatment goes okay for you."

"Thanks!" She took the money and popped it into her purse before he could change his mind.

"I'll come back and pick Kieran up about six-ish if that's alright? We've got Marie's parents over for tea this afternoon. It'll be an excuse to escape."

"Fine; make sure Kevin's got all the clothes he'll need and his Playstation."

"Yeah; will do. So long for now. Have a nice lunch."

"Ta." She smiled at him as he turned to wave before opening the garden gate.

"What can you afford on the menu, Mum?" Kevin turned around and whispered as he followed the waiter to their table.

"Anything, now Dad's paying." Erin's broken voice whispered back, and she grinned.

"Great! Can I have one of those T-bone steaks and a bucket of chips then?"

"Be my guest, but I don't want to listen to you whining with the guts ache all night though."

"I won't."

"He will, Mum. He's greedy."

"Shut up, turd boy." Kevin whispered to his brother *sotto voce.*

"I'm going to have the biggest pizza the chef can cook." Kieran sat down and picked up a menu. "It's going to have everything on it and be as big as the table."

"Good God; you'll be up all night as well then. You'll be popular with Marie." Erin looked over the selections. "They haven't got pizza. This is a bit more upmarket than the usual greasy spoon cafes you boys like. Think of something else."

"I'll have the same as tur…..Kevin; T-bone and chips." Kieran pointed to his choice on the menu.

"Okay. You order; my voice is squeaking. Whatever you boys want, and mine is trout, new potatoes and vegetables. Ask for a glass of water for me, and whatever soft drinks you two want."

"Can I have a pint of lager?" Kieran looked towards his mother hopefully.

"Don't push your luck, Buster. Make it two cokes." She managed what she thought was quite a sizeable glare in her son's direction.

"Dad lets us have half a pint of lager each with our Sunday lunch." Kieran looked towards his brother, and the two nodded as one.

"Oh, he does, does he? Well, I'll have to have a word with him about that." Erin signalled to the waiter and made a mental note to tackle Chris on the subject when he picked Kieran up at teatime.

# CHAPTER 27

"YOU'LL BE ALRIGHT; you don't like fishy things anyway." Matilda gave Alan back the piece of paper. "We can have loads of chicken dishes, beef or turkey. Matty and I are going to look after you."

"I don't need looking after. I'm quite capable of managing on my own." Alan bridled with indignation. "I don't want anybody feeling sorry for me."

"I say make the most of the attention while it lasts." Matilda gave her father a kiss. "Matty's coming over ready for the last supper tonight. I'm cooking a big cheesy lasagne. Your new diet starts tomorrow doesn't it?"

"Yeah. I've got to stop taking the tablets as well after today."

"What'll happen when you do?" Matilda looked at her father questioningly.

"Apparently I'll fold up into a ball and sink down on the settee, never to get up again."

"No you won't; you'll still be down the garage at six o'clock every morning."

"You bet I will; I ain't finished yet." Alan gave Matilda a weak thumbs up sign.

"When do you need to go for your treatment?" Matilda took the instructions back from her father and re-scanned the page.

"Nineteenth of October. Woop-de-do; can't wait." Alan sighed.

"We'll be rooting for you, Dad." Matilda opened the fridge door and took out a packet of mince. "I'm going to put some extra cheese in this just for you."

His upcoming treatment hanging like a black cloud above his head, and at a loss of how to spend the rest of his Sunday afternoon until dinner, Alan fell asleep in his favourite armchair, only rising when he heard the doorbell ringing.

"Lover boy's arrived." Alan staggered into the kitchen, seated himself at the kitchen table and uncorked a bottle of wine. "You'd better go and let him in; he won't want to see me."

"Of course he will; don't talk wet." Matilda wiped her hands on her apron and walked into the hallway. "Don't drink the whole bottle while I'm away."

Alan felt like drinking many bottles of wine all at the same time. He craved the oblivion of an alcohol-induced sleep, and the chance to blot out the grim reality of his life even for a short time. By the time he heard Tilly and Matthew return he had managed to empty a third of the bottle.

"I'd better dish up to soak up some of that alcohol." Matilda put on some protective gloves, opened the oven door, and took out a steaming tray of lasagne.

"Smells good!" Matthew rubbed his hands together. "How's it going, Alan?"

"Peachy." Alan grimaced and topped up his glass. "Don't worry; you'll be fine. The garage will run like clockwork while you're away. I solved that Mondeo's alarm problem by the way. Water had got into that little battery unit in the wheel arch. Matthew sat himself down opposite Alan at the table.

"That's a weight off my mind." Alan sighed and took another sip of wine.

"Dad; will you stop feeling sorry for yourself? There's plenty worse off than you." Matilda glared at her father, plonked three dinner plates on the placemats with some force, and placed the tray of lasagne on a cork mat in the middle of the table, together with an oven dish of roasted vegetables.

"Lovely!" Matthew eyed the lasagne appreciatively. "Thanks Tilly, this is great."

"It's Dad's last treat for a few weeks; let's make it a good night." Matilda sat down, poured herself some wine, and raised her glass. "To Dad; in a few weeks you'll be as good as new again!"

"To Alan!" Matthew clinked his glass with Alan's, and then with Matilda's.

"Cheers guys. It all smells very tempting; let's tuck in." Alan put down his wine glass and ladled food onto his plate in an enthusiastic a manner as he could manage.

"There's half term at college the week after you come home from hospital." Matilda helped herself to more vegetables. "I'll be able to help you more around the house then."

"You'd best do your college work instead of running around after me. It's your last year now isn't it?" Alan put down his knife and fork and looked over at his daughter.

"Yes, but all I'll have to practise is getting my typing speed up a bit more and a little bit more practical work to do with word processing. I thought the advanced secretarial course was going to be hard, but it's not too bad really."

"Good for you; you'll be the smartest PA of them all." Alan smiled and took another sip of wine.

"Well, I've got to get a job first."

"You'll get one; no doubt about that."

Matilda took a deep breath, and Alan saw the quick glance dart between her and Matthew:

"Dad."

"What?" Alan had a nasty feeling something was coming at him right below the belt.

"Matty and I want to get engaged."

Alan nearly choked on his drink.

"Engaged? You're only eighteen! You've only known each other a few months!" He looked from one to the other of them with an open mouth.

"I love her. There's nobody else for me except Tilly." Matthew reached across the table and took hold of Matilda's hand.

"I'm nearly nineteen, Dad. I'm grown up; it's what I want. We're sleeping together now; I need you to be happy for me." Matilda looked beseechingly at her father for approval.

Alan knew when he was beaten. He closed his mouth, picked up his fork with his left hand, and held his right hand out towards Matthew.

"Congratulations. Welcome to the family, son."

# CHAPTER 28

ERIN FELT A bit of a fraud for being off work. Three days into the pre-treatment regime, and she felt no ill-effects at all from the lack of her T3 tablets. She was aware that Kevin was hanging about more in the evenings instead of cycling about with his friends, but she had no problems preparing food, cooking, or doing the housework. Even Kieran had biked round the previous afternoon on finishing college, but had constantly been giving her strange, quick surreptitious glances, and had even cut the grass without being asked.

It was not until the second Monday that the lack of thyroxine started to bite. She realised she felt weary even though she had not long got out of bed, and she started to get pains in her calf muscles when she tried to clean around the house with the vacuum cleaner. Her eyes felt as though they had lead weights on the lids holding them down. She had no appetite, but was gaining weight. She looked at herself in the mirror, and was appalled on seeing a pale, puffy moon face staring back.

"Mum, you're shuffling about like an old woman." Kevin snatched the duster and polish out of his mother's hands on the second Saturday.

"It hurts to walk." Erin whispered, and wanted to cry with misery.

"Then sit down. That's what I'm here for."

"You shouldn't be doing things for me; it's supposed to be the other way around."

"Just give in. You're only like this because you've stopped your tablets don't forget."

Erin let her son lead her to the settee, where she sank down gratefully. She had no energy at all, and could never remember ever feeling so bad. She kept having to fight a constant urge to burst into tears.

"I'll make you a nice cup of tea. Dad's texted to ask how you are. Nan keeps phoning my mobile, but I'm still managing to put her off. She's coming early Monday morning though to take you into hospital. I can't change that."

Erin smiled weakly. Her body was giving up on her, and suddenly she cared not two hoots about anything. She was happy to let Kevin take charge.

"Thanks for everything." She put her head on a cushion and drifted off to sleep.

Less than five miles away and also on that second Saturday, Alan Beaumont felt like absolute shit. He had grudgingly given up his garage keys to Matthew after struggling to even get out of bed, let alone trying to drive to work. His legs hurt whenever he tried to walk, his eyes were not focusing properly, and although Matilda was putting all kinds of tempting foods his way, he could hardly eat a thing.

"Matty's driving you to hospital on Monday because I'll be at college. Do you think we ought to tell Mum what's going on?" Matilda looked down at the supine form of her father laid out on the settee.

"Why? What does she care? She's with Doofer the Roofer now, or whatever his name is." Alan could not keep the bitterness out of his voice.

"You *were* married once."

"Well, now we're not. Does she keep phoning your mobile then?" Alan could hardly summon the energy to open his eyes.

"Not very often, but she's obviously still trying to keep in touch with me. I'm not really interested in becoming her bosom buddy though; I haven't even told her I'm engaged." Matilda shrugged her shoulders.

"It's up to you what you do about Mum of course, but I'm finished with it all." Alan tried to focus on his daughter's face and wondered if he was losing his sight.

"Okay; I won't tell her anything. She left us, so she can't complain if she learns it second-hand from somebody else."

"Too bloody right......." Alan dozed off in the middle of a sentence.

# CHAPTER 29

"HELLO ERIN; MY name is Ann Wilkes; I'm the manager of the Radioiodine suite. I'll give you half an hour or so to get settled in and unpack your things, and then I'll take some admission details from you. A doctor will be along soon to take some blood; we need to check your thyroglobulin, haemoglobin, and thyroid stimulating hormone levels. You'll have your treatment after lunch, and you'll be given an anti-sickness pill about half an hour beforehand. Any questions?"

Erin tried to rest her gaze on the kindly older lady who was smiling at her, but felt too tired to do anything other than sit in the armchair, let her eyelids droop, and shake her head. She was aware that her mother was uncharacteristically silent for once, as she bustled around the room unpacking clothes, puzzle books and snacks.

"Good. Settle in then, and I'll see you soon."

After nurse Wilkes had departed, Erin forced her eyelids to stay open as she focused with some difficulty on her surroundings. The room seemed quite small, with a large double glazed windows taking up the upper part of the outside wall. Underneath a long, flat windowsill was a workbench which ran the length of the wall. Erin noticed a sink and tea making facilities in one corner of the bench, and a fridge and rubbish bin underneath it. Next to her armchair she could see that a well-equipped hospital bed complete with adjustment controls and a nurse call button was the main feature of the room, with a medium-sized wall-mounted television screen opposite. A telephone and a remote control for the TV rested on top of a cabinet situated on the other side of the bed. To the right of the entrance another door led off to what she supposed was the bathroom. As though by telepathy she heard her mother's voice through her closed eyelids.

"Yes, it is a bathroom. There's a toilet, sink and walk-in shower in there. It's all very clean and well-kept. Did I tell you about the cockroaches I found in the bathroom when I had my hysterectomy?"

Erin nodded. She must have heard the story at least five hundred times. She wanted her mother to leave her alone in peace to wallow in her misery.

"You'll need to go now, Mum. Thanks for the lift, but I don't think you're supposed to stay." Erin whispered and opened her eyes with difficulty.

"If you're sure? I'll be back to pick you up as soon as you ring."

"Yeah, I'm sure. Thanks for everything." She offered up a silent prayer of relief.

She smelt expensive perfume as her mother bent over to give her a kiss:

"Good luck, darling. Keep in touch. There's a telephone by your bed."

"I know; I'll phone as soon as I can."

"Bye for now."

"Bye Mum." Erin fought back tears as her mother picked up her bag, opened the entrance door, and walked out. "Thanks again."

"All settled?" Ann Wilkes popped her head around the door.

"Yes thanks." Erin nodded and tried to raise a smile. "I'll come in now and admit you, and then after your blood tests you can have some lunch."

Ann carried with her a sheaf of papers in a folder. She sat herself down on the bed, took out the first form, and fished around inside the folder for a pen.

"Can I just check your name, address and date of birth please?"

"Erin Elaine Mason; twenty four St. Faith's Close, Goldmark Estate. Date of birth August second nineteen seventy."

"Great, and your GP?"

"Doctor Draper at the Goldmark surgery." "Do you live in a house or a flat on the estate?"

"In a two-bedroomed maisonette with my twin sons. I'm divorced."

"And you're okay with the stairs?"

"Well not lately because of stopping my tablets, but usually yes."

"I see. So who is your next of kin please?"

"My mother Cynthia Parry. I have her contact details." Erin scrabbled about in her handbag and handed over a piece of paper. "Here's her telephone numbers."

"Thank you." Ann Wilkes copied down the information and handed the page back. "Any allergies that you know of?"

"No."

Thanks Erin; I'll just attach this wristband to you, and then you're ready for your blood tests. The doctor is just outside, so I'll let him come in while I admit the other patient for treatment next door."

Within a few moments of the nurse's departure, Erin heard another knock. Without waiting for a reply, the door flew open and a rather harassed-looking young doctor appeared.

"Ms Mason; I need to take some blood from you. We need to check various baseline levels before your treatment."

"Go ahead." Erin sighed and held out her arm.

"After lunch you will be given your anti-sickness pill." The doctor expertly applied a tourniquet.

"Is the food that bad then?" Erin attempted a feeble joke to lighten the atmosphere.

"Ha; it can be." The doctor smiled. "No, this will be to make sure that the radioactive iodine stays down for at least the two to three hours it needs to be absorbed by your body. After that you will need to drink lots of water and take as many showers as you can to flush it out of your system."

"I see."

Erin watched as her blood flowed into a syringe.

"When can I go home again?" She felt miserable at the thought of being holed up alone in the tiny room for days on end.

"When radioactive levels in your body are safe for you to be let out into the community. The physicist will check the levels on the second and subsequent days. The more you drink and wash, the quicker it'll be that we let you out." The doctor removed the needle and the tourniquet.

"I'll be washing myself away then." Erin whispered and managed a smile whilst stemming the flow of blood by pressing down on the crook of her arm with a piece of cotton wool.

"That's the idea. Of course you know to stay in the room once you have had your treatment. There's an alarm outside the suite that is triggered by radiation. If you come out you'll set it off."

"No; don't worry. I'll stay here. I can hardly walk about at the moment."

"That's only temporary. Next week you can start your thyroxine again, and you'll soon feel better."

"I hope so. I feel like death warmed up at the moment." She whispered and closed her eyes.

"I'll leave you now and bother the other new patient next door. The physicist Margaret Baines, will come by soon to check your identity, and Laura, one of the housekeepers, will come and enquire whether you would like any newspapers. You'll have to give her the money today though."

"Okay, thanks." Erin wished everyone would go and leave her in peace.

# CHAPTER 30

HE DOZED AGAIN in the armchair after being admitted, but then awoke to another knock. He looked down at his arm; the irritating plastic wristband was looser than it should be, and he felt like sliding it off.

"Come in!"

"Hi; I'm Margaret Baines, the physicist. I'm going to administer your radioactive iodine round about half past two. I just need to check your details." A pleasant middle-aged lady stood at the door clad in a white coat.

"Someone called Ann Wilkes did that about half an hour ago." Alan sighed and wished they'd all piss off.

"I'm afraid I need to do it again."

"Whatever floats your boat, love."

The physicist looked at her clipboard and then at the wristband.

"Can you confirm your name, address and date of birth please?"

"Alan Robert Beaumont. Address is twelve Moffat Court, Leas Road. Date of birth is January eighteenth nineteen sixty three." Alan found that her face moved in and out of focus as he spoke.

"And who is your next of kin?"

"My daughter Matilda Beaumont; same address and phone number."

"Thank you." Margaret smiled. "Has the procedure been explained to you?"

"Yeah; the doctor who took my blood went through it."

"I'll just add that I'll bring the radioiodine drink around half past two. It'll arrive in a lead-lined box, and you will drink it through a straw. You'll need to drink lots of water afterwards and take as many showers as you like to flush it out of your system."

"Yeah; I know. The doc explained it." Alan was tired and wanted to sleep; the constant interruptions were beginning to get on his tits.

Margaret Baines wrote in her notes, and then stood up.

"Have a nice lunch; I'll see you later."

"Yeah." Alan was asleep before she had walked out of the door.

"Will you want any newspapers?"

He woke again with a start. The clock on the wall in front of him showed that only ten minutes had passed since the physicist had left, and now a young solidly-built woman of about thirty five was standing over him. He had not even heard her come in.

"I'm Laura, the housekeeper. Have you got enough towels and pillows? There's plenty on the unit if you would like more. If you want newspapers while you're here you'll have to give me the money now and I'll put them through the hatch each morning."

Alan fished in the pocket of his jeans. Earlier he had given Tilly some money for shopping, and was not sure how much he had left. When opening his wallet his woolly brain was pleased to discover there were still fifteen pounds left.

"Yeah; can I have a Daily Mail every morning please? I've got enough pillows, but I haven't been in the bathroom yet to check if I've got any towels." He put three pound coins on the bedside table in front of him.

"No probs; I'll do that." Laura pocketed the money and popped her head around the bathroom door. "There's loads of towels in there. I'll put your change through the hatch every morning with the newspaper."

"Ta." Alan's patience was wearing thin.

"It's lamb stew or cauliflower cheese for lunch."

"Lamb stew please. I'm not allowed to eat cheese." He masked his surprise at being offered dairy produce.

"They bring the hot locks round at one o'clock. I'll bring your lunch in today, but will put the rest of your meals through the hatch. We'll ring the phone on your bedside cabinet before meals and check what you would like to eat, or you can fill in some menus beforehand." Laura held a blank menu up for inspection.

"Cheers. Call me on the phone and I'll tell you what I want." Alan closed his eyes and prayed for peace and quiet.

"Lunch, Mr Beaumont!"

Alan nearly fell out of his chair. While he had dozed, the hands of the clock had moved around to ten past one, and Laura was now standing in front of him with a steaming plate of lamb stew. Alan yawned and sat up straighter in his chair. He wondered if he was going to be interrupted every half an hour during the night as well.

"Ta, darlin'. Put it on the table."

"I'm not allowed to collect any plates now. Just wash it under the tap and leave it on the table by the hatch."

Laura's sturdy form exited the room, and Alan could hear her knocking on another door nearby. He settled down to eat the stew, which was hot and tasty and contained just the right amount of garlic. He had just finished eating it when to his dismay there was another knock on the door.

"Yeah?" He started to wonder whether there was any point having a door to the room at all.

"Just bringing round your anti-sickness pill." Ann Wilkes held out a small paper container. "Please can you take this."

"Sure." Alan took the pill from the container and swallowed it with a sip of water. "Don't want to lose the lamb stew do I?" He yawned and looked up at the nurse.

"Absolutely not. Your last visitor of the day will be Margaret Baines with the radioiodine in about half an hour."

"Bring it on." Alan closed his eyes and fell into a fitful doze.

# CHAPTER 31

ERIN RINSED HER plate in the sink and cleaned her knife and fork. Her tired brain had forgotten that she was not supposed to eat cauliflower cheese, but the lunch had been delicious and for once she had been hungry. She placed her plate out on the table in the little lobby by the hatch as she had been instructed to do. The sound of snoring could be heard coming from the room next door. Erin wished for the oblivion of sleep, and hoped the many interruptions of the morning were now coming to an end.

At exactly half past two her heart started to beat wildly in her chest on hearing Margaret Baines' voice in the outside lobby, but when nobody knocked on her door Erin realised the physicist had probably visited the patient in the next room first. Muted sounds could be heard through the wall; Margaret's high tones and a louder, deeper male voice. Erin sat with her stomach in knots, waiting for the drink that would attack the unseen enemy in her neck, but might also give her leukaemia in the years to come.

Towards three o'clock the fateful knock occurred. Erin could only whisper, and so shuffled over to the door and opened it.

"Good afternoon Ms Mason. It's time for your radioiodine drink."

Margaret Baines stepped inside the room carrying an impossibly large bottle, and Erin's face fell.

"Good God! Have I got to drink all that?" She looked aghast at the bottle.

"That's what the other patient just said, although not as politely." Margaret laughed. "No, you will need to pour some of this down the toilet just before you flush it, which will help to break up the radiation. My assistant has the drink."

Erin looked behind Margaret to where a young man in his twenties came into the room carrying a small container.

"We need to check your identity bracelet once more please."

Margaret came in closer as Erin stretched out her arm. Satisfied, the physicist put on a plastic apron.

"Here's an apron for you, Ms Mason, to guard against splashes."

Erin secured the plastic apron around her, and watched as the assistant inserted two needles into the top of the small phial of radioiodine sitting in its protective lead-lined case. She then noticed the needles being attached to two plastic tubes.

"One of these tubes you drink out of like a straw, and the other one we'll put into a cup of water which will help to flush all of the radioiodine out of the phial and into you. Drink it slowly and carefully, and try not to splash any of the liquid anywhere."

With her heart threatening to jump out of her chest, Erin sucked up the cool, tasteless drink in no time at all. Margaret and her assistant expertly packed up the equipment and aprons, and took the first radiation reading with a Geiger counter.

"Radiation levels will need to be a quarter of what they are now before you can go home. Start drinking in about half an hour, and have a shower later on." Margaret smiled and signalled to her assistant to open the door.

"Thanks. Will do." Erin yawned and sat back in her chair.

When left alone Erin waited for something to happen, but nothing did. She waited to feel sick, but fortunately felt quite normal. After the regulation half an hour she filled a cup with water from the sink and drank from it. She tried to drink another cupful but felt too bloated, so she shuffled back to her armchair, closed her eyes, and slept.

The noise of the television in the room next door pervaded her dreams. Erin woke up some time later, and for a brief moment wondered where she was. The clock opposite showed twenty minutes to five; her eyelids and limbs felt heavy, and there was a slight metallic taste in her mouth. Ignoring the pain from her complaining calf muscles, she stood up and shuffled over to the sink to fill up the kettle and make a cup of tea. The noise from the commentators and the crowd at what sounded like a football match in the next room was extremely irritating, and invaded her peace and quiet.

When the kettle boiled she swirled a herbal teabag around in some boiling water. Just as she put the cup to her lips the phone rang. Moving as fast as she could with the cup in one hand, she shuffled over to the bedside cabinet and picked up the receiver.

"Ms Mason, this is Housekeeping; what would you like for supper tonight? There's some soup and sandwiches, or pasta and Bolognese sauce."

"Soup and sandwiches please; brown bread if possible." Erin was quite pleased to speak to even a disembodied voice.

"Okay. Will ring the bell at the hatch when it's ready for you."

She heard the phone ringing in the next room, and the pleasantly deep, resonant tones of a male voice answering. She wondered whether to knock on his door and introduce herself, but then thought better of it. She turned on the TV and channel-hopped with the remote control until she found a mindless quiz show to drown out the sound of the football commentary.

The bell sounded quite loud in the outside lobby. Erin jumped up as fast as her suffering body would allow, and made her way out of the room to the hatch. As she lifted the hatch door and peered inside, she was aware that the door to the other room had opened behind her.

"Mine's the pasta and Bolognese sauce."

She looked around to find a pleasant looking middle-aged man standing around six feet tall, with thick greying hair and a day's stubble on his chin, who gave the outward impression of having been out on the tiles for the past few sleepless nights.

"You look as rough as I feel." Erin whispered, smiled at him, and passed him a tray of food.

"When I was eighteen I used to feel like this on a Sunday morning, but at least I'd been trolleyed the previous night and had a good time." Alan peered with distaste at the bowl of pasta. "You don't get much for your money do you?"

"My appetite's shot anyway. These two sarnies and the soup will do for me." Erin picked up her tray. "Hi; I'm Erin Mason. I feel like I've been run over by a bus if that's any consolation."

"No consolation whatever, but nice to meet you. I'm Alan Beaumont; fat, fifty, and fucked up."

"Yeah; join the club, although I've not reached fifty yet." Erin chuckled.

"Lucky old you. Anyway, it's all happening in my room if you want to bring your supper in?" Alan peered again at the small bowl of pasta, yawned, and then looked over at Erin.

"Why not? Nobody else wants to know us. We're unclean." Erin whispered. "I'll come in then and join the party.

# CHAPTER 32

"SO WHAT'S WITH the whispering then?"

Alan looked up from his armchair and twirled some pasta around on his fork, gazing with interest at the good-looking red-headed fortysomething woman perched on the edge of his bed.

"When I woke up from the anaesthetic I had no voice." Erin swallowed a mouthful of sandwich. "I'm hoping it'll come back; they say it will. I don't think the op was an easy one, and maybe one of the vocal cords were damaged. Who knows?" She panted for breath and shrugged her shoulders.

"Sue the surgeon." Alan nodded to emphasise his point.

"Hmm; don't know about that. Does your pasta taste funny?" Erin wrinkled her nose. "I keep tasting something metallic."

"It tastes like shit." Alan sighed while putting another forkful of pasta into his mouth.

"That's just hospital food probably." Erin grimaced. "My eyes keep wanting to close."

"You and me both. I'm walking like an old man. This treatment sucks. I felt better with the cancer." Alan stifled a yawn and toyed with his fork.

Erin finished her sandwiches and inspected the bowl of soup.

"I wonder what flavour this is? She looked quizzically at the indeterminate hue of the viscous liquid.

"What did they say it was?"

"They didn't; they just said soup and sandwiches." She sipped a spoonful. "Ugh, it tastes of metal."

"Do you fancy some cake? My daughter made something spongy and put it in my bag. It's got to taste better than this." Alan put his fork down in disgust and stood up slowly. "I put it in the fridge. Hang on, I'll get it." He winced with pain as he walked very gingerly over to the fridge and opened the door.

"Unfortunately I never got around to training my sons to make cakes; how old is she?" Erin gazed appreciatively at the perfect-looking jam sponge topped with icing sugar.

"She'll be nineteen at the end of next month; makes me feel old. She's just told me she's going to get engaged; I still can't believe it." Alan fished in a drawer under the worktop and brought out a knife. "Shall I cut you a piece?"

"Yes please; it looks lovely. My twin boys are sixteen; they're more interested in girls now than cooking."

"Yep; I can understand that. Here you are; Tilly's a great little cook." Alan cut some cake and passed it to Erin on a plate.

"Thanks. One of my boys has been looking after me this last week, but he's back staying with his dad now until I'm fit again." Erin bit into a delicious, moist sponge.

Erin saw a flicker of interest pass across Alan's pale face.

"Ah; so you're a member of the Divorced and Separated club as well then?"

"Yeah, for three years." Erin nodded. "Chris went off with the lovely Marie; he's got another son as well now."

"Tina went off with the chap who came to mend our roof. I was at work all day slogging my guts out in the garage, and Marvin was having a quick up and under as well as an even quicker up and over, charging me five hundred pounds for the privilege."

Erin wanted to laugh, but thought better of it. She bit her lip and kept a straight face.

"Life; you never know what's coming round the corner do you?"

"No, you don't. Now I've got the wonderful Matty as a prospective son-in-law, with his foot in the door of my garage just waiting for me to kick the bucket." Alan tried unsuccessfully to keep the bitterness out of his voice. "Me and Tilly have been fine on our own for four years, but now it seems to be Tilly and Matty instead."

"It's the way of things; sooner or later the chicks fly the nest." Erin smiled. "Consider you've done a good job as a dad, and let her go. I've heard they soon come back again when they want you to babysit. Have you got other children?"

"No; just Tilly." Alan yawned again. "I can't keep awake. I'm afraid I'm going to have to get in the shower and then hit the sack."

"Yes, I must do the same. Thanks for the company." Erin got to her feet. "I'm going to speak to my boys and my mum first though on the phone; well, try to speak anyway."

"I'll knock for you tomorrow to see if you're coming out to play." Alan took the plate from Erin's outstretched hand.

"Ta; this whole palaver seems more tolerable with someone else who's in the same boat."

"Yeah; see you by the hatch in the morning; it's the new place to hang out."

Erin felt somewhat lighter in mood as she shuffled back to her room. She looked at her door handle, but could not see any lock. However, for some reason she knew that under his somewhat gruff exterior Alan would be the perfect gentleman. She closed the little blind in the viewing window, and switched on the light. She felt quite safe.

# CHAPTER 33

THE SOUND OF retching woke him from a fitful sleep. Alan wondered whether to get out of bed and investigate, but was held back at first by etiquette and by his mother's imbued high moral stance that no gentleman would ever go knocking on a strange lady's door in the middle of the night.

Eventually after half an hour had passed, he could stand it no longer. Kicking himself as he climbed out of bed for not thinking he might ever need a pair of pyjamas at some point in his life, he tied the cord of his dressing gown tightly around his waist to cover his nakedness, and with a rapidly beating heart he cleaned his teeth and moved towards the door as quickly as his painful calf muscles would allow.

Out in the lobby he could see that her room was ablaze with light through the slats in the window blind. Summoning up all his courage he rapped smartly on the window.

"Erin, it's Alan! Are you okay?"

Within a few moments the door opened to reveal a vision of unloveliness in pink stripy pyjamas. At that precise moment he thought he had never seen anybody looking so green around the gills in all his life.

"Sorry to bother you; I just knocked to see if I could be of any help."

He was suddenly aware of not having any trousers on, and his dressing gown not totally covering his white hairy legs and similarly hirsute toes. With some regret he wished he'd given in and let Tilly pack for him; at least then he would have had some slippers on his feet.

"I phoned the desk and asked for another anti-sickness tablet. Could you see if they've put it in the hatch please?" Erin whispered and covered her mouth with one hand.

"Sure."

He checked in the hatch as she turned to hurry back into the bathroom. There was a lone paper receptacle at the other end, and he reached in to grab it. He could see it contained just one small white tablet. Treating it as though it were the Crown jewels he carried it carefully and walked through the open door towards the sounds of gagging.

"Here you go; see if you can keep this down."

She smiled weakly and stood up from her kneeling position over the toilet bowl.

"Thanks." She took the tablet from him and swallowed it, after flushing the toilet and rinsing with mouthwash. "I told you that soup tasted funny."

"Don't forget you're supposed to pour some of the stuff out of that bottle down the loo." Alan indicated towards a large brown bottle on the floor.

"Oh, bloody hell; I forgot." She whispered. "I'll put some down now and flush it again." Erin picked up the bottle and took off the lid.

"Perhaps they gave you more radiation than they gave me? I feel okay." Alan could see a tinge of colour coming back to her cheeks.

"I don't know; all I do know is that I feel like shit." Erin flushed the system again, closed the lid of the toilet seat, and sank down upon it gratefully. "So sorry to wake you up; I couldn't help it."

"It's okay; no problem. I'll make you a cup of tea if you like?" He was grateful for the chance to be able to do something.

"That'll be nice; thanks. Make yourself one too; I'll just sit here for a while and try to keep hold of the pill."

"Milk and sugar?"

"Yeah, great."

He stole a surreptitious glance around the room as he waited for the kettle to boil. On her bedside cabinet he could see a photo of two smiling and identical red-headed teenage boys sitting in a double canoe.

"How do you tell your boys apart?" He washed two cups at the sink and plonked in two teabags.

"It's easy; there's several ways for someone who's never met them. Kevin has a white patch on one of his front teeth, and he's also the quieter one. Kieran has more freckles and he's a nutter." Erin wandered out from the bathroom and picked up the photo.

"I've never seen two boys so identical." Alan chuckled as he poured hot water into the cups. "You're looking a bit better now."

"Yeah, that tablet seems to be working, not that there's much to come up now anyway." Erin took the teabag out of her cup and added some milk from the fridge. "Do you want some milk?"

"Just a little bit please." He held out his cup.

"It's no good trying to impress somebody when you're having this treatment, is it?" Erin giggled and sipped some tea.

"Aren't you supposed to be dressed to kill, with shovelfuls of makeup on and not a hair out of place?" Alan smiled and perched on the end of the bed.

"At three o'clock in the morning? No chance! I can truthfully say you've caught me at my utter worst." Erin slumped in the armchair and wrapped her hands around the warm cup.

"Well, I'm hardly a walking Adonis either." Alan sighed and swung his legs to and fro before jumping off the bed. "Tell you what; let's start again in the morning. I'm going back to bed now; thanks for the tea and glad you're feeling better."

"Cheers; see you by the hatch at breakfast. I'll try to look more human by then." Erin smiled and raised one hand to wave at him.

He was grinning as he made his way back to bed.

# CHAPTER 34

"DON'T TELL ME; you've ordered a greasy bacon roll, greasy fried bread, and three fried eggs." Alan chuckled as he opened the hatch.

"I feel sick again just thinking about that combination." Erin made a face. "No; there should be a bowl of cereal and some toast arrived?" She looked questioningly towards him.

"Yep; get that down you and you'll be raring to go again." He handed over her breakfast tray.

"I wish; I've been asleep for the last five hours but I feel exhausted again after having a shower." Erin yawned and walked towards her room. "The party's in here this morning if you'd care to join me?"

"Why not?" Alan picked up his tray and followed behind Erin, glad for the chance to have had a proper shower and shave, and to be decently dressed.

"Perch on the bed again if you like; it's a shame there's only one armchair."

"I noticed a little cupboard outside. I'll just go and see what's in it; perhaps there's some chairs for visitors."

Alan put his tray down on the bed and went out to the lobby.

"Yeah, there's a few fold up chairs in here. I'll bring one in." He reappeared carrying what looked like a plastic garden seat.

"Great; the beds aren't too comfortable for sitting on, are they?" Erin chewed on some cereal, disappointed to find the metallic taste still present.

"This is better; at least I can rest the tray on my lap properly." Alan sniffed at his plate appreciatively. "Sausages, scrambled eggs and beans; the best way to start a day. I'm going to eat all of this even though I'm not that hungry."

"That's what my boys would say, although it seems they're always famished. It must be something to do with the male psyche." Erin whispered and screwed up her nose. "Just give me cereal and toast."

"Tilly always wants me to eat porridge and pumpkin seeds. I tell her pumpkin seeds are for parrots, but I could use cold porridge to plaster the walls of my garage with." Alan dug his knife into a succulent sausage.

"She sounds a sensible girl." Erin chuckled.

"Eighteen going on forty; Matty's a lucky bloke." Alan's face fell. "Thinking about it, he's probably moved in now while I've been stuck here."

"You can't stop young love. You'll only turn her away if you start laying down the law." Erin buttered some toast and took a bite. "If she's happy then good for her."

"You're right, I know. It's just that yesterday she was my little girl; my princess." Alan's eyes took on a faraway look.

"She'll always be your little girl, but you have to let her grow up. I keep thinking back to when my boys were small, but it doesn't do any good. We have to look to the future and move on." Erin shrugged her shoulders. "Oh, I think somebody's just come in."

They looked towards the door as it opened to reveal the white-coated form of Dr Ingram.

"Hi; I see you two are already becoming acquainted. I'm just popping my head briefly around the door to make sure you're both okay?" He looked from one to the other.

"I've been sick in the night, but I'm feeling a bit better now, although still tired." Erin put down her spoon and buttered another slice of toast.

"Nausea is a side-effect of the treatment unfortunately, and you'll probably feel tired for another couple of weeks until your thyroxine levels come back up. How about you, Mr Beaumont?"

"Like Erin, tired but not too bad."    Alan nodded as he ate.

"Today's Tuesday; I expect you'll both be able to go home either tomorrow or Thursday. You'll be okay to start your thyroxine tablets again tomorrow, but you'll both need to come back on Friday for a Gamma scan. Margaret Baines will be around about half past two to check on the radiation levels."

"Cheers; thanks doc." Alan waved in salutation as the oncologist disappeared back into the outside lobby.

"It seems funny to see another person in the room, doesn't it?" Erin smiled. "Do you want a cup of tea? I'll put the kettle on."

"He's brave, what with all the radiation flying about. Yeah, some tea would be good, please. I'll get my milk if you like, to save using up yours."

"I've got enough for a few days." Erin put her tray on the floor and stood up. "Isn't it strange? We can't see the cancer and we can't see the treatment either."

"Sometimes I wonder if I'm having a nightmare and nothing's real." Alan reached up to touch the front of his neck. "This scar's real, so I must have had cancer. I'm still trying to get my head around the whole thing."

"Yeah, it's scary I'll admit. I keep thinking I'm going to die, but I didn't feel ill until I had this treatment." Erin walked over to the kettle and switched it on. "I worry that I won't be around for my boys. They're staying with their dad, but I know they'd rather be home."

"I've got a lot of living to do yet; I want to give my daughter away at her wedding." Alan tried to keep the desperation out of his voice.

"You will; you just need to go through this thing first." Erin washed up two cups from the night before. "I've been told the cancer's treatable; the trouble is the mind runs away with itself and you end up thinking the worst when you're stuck here on your own."

"At least you're not pissing yourself laughing at me." Alan sighed.

"Why would I laugh? I've got fears, just like you." Erin poured boiling water into the cups and put a teabag in each one. "It's nothing to be ashamed about." "Yeah, we're in the same boat."

"My ex-husband would never talk about *anything*. I think he saw it as a sign of weakness. He'd been seeing Marie for two years before I found out." She took the teabags out, and added some milk and sugar.

"Christ; Tina told me almost straight away. I never saw it coming though; I tend to go around with my head in the sand. Ta for the brew." Alan took a cup. "Tilly didn't want anything more to do with her mum, although Tina's trying to win her around now that she's older."

"Your daughter must make up her own mind of course. My ex has to pay for the boys' upkeep, so he always has access. They get on well, and I didn't want to spoil their relationship with their dad."

"Fair enough. I could never get Tilly to visit her mum; hardly surprising really. Tina left when Tilly was at a vulnerable age. It's amazing how great the kid's turned out though." Alan shook his head in wonder.

"Sounds like you're a good Dad." Erin smiled and sipped her tea.

"Who knows? We've become close over the years, but now I have to get used to lover boy."

"Inevitable; if he's good to her then she's a lucky girl."

"He works for me in my garage. She popped round after college for a chat one day. I was up at the post office and the rest, as they say, is history." Alan sniffed. "The glands feel swollen in my neck; how about yours?"

"Not too bad; my mouth's dry though. I want to keep drinking."

"We're supposed to drink lots anyway, to flush it all out. Come on; I'll wash the breakfast plates and you can dry. It'll give us something to do." Alan stood up slowly and picked up the trays. "I'm getting cabin fever."

"Already?"

"Yeah. I'm used to being busy and working, not sitting around doing nothing."

"I don't know about you, but I'm going back to sleep for a bit when we've washed up."

"Okay; I'll leave you in peace in a mo; give us a knock when you wake up."

"Will do."

As he washed up the plates and gave them to Erin to dry, Alan had the strangest thought that while occupied in doing the most mundane chore together it seemed as though he had known her for much longer than just one day.

# CHAPTER 35

ERIN WOKE UP and for a brief moment wondered where she was. The clock opposite showed ten minutes past eleven. She was lying fully clothed on top of the bedclothes, and the muted sounds of rhythmic snoring could be heard coming from the room next door.

She sat up, rubbed her eyes, and looked around the room. The cups and plates they had washed up after breakfast sat in a pile on the worktop, and the plastic chair that Alan had brought in from the lobby earlier that morning sat forlorn in one corner of the room where she had moved it to.

In the silence of her room she remembered the printed instructions and decided to have another shower. Shuffling to the bathroom she undressed and turned on the mixer tap, enjoying the sensation of warm water pummelling her skin. She felt pleased to be able to do something physical, and to literally be able to wash the radiation away from her body.

Feeling cleansed and refreshed, Erin put on some new clothes and combed her hair. She hung up the towels to dry and walked back into the main living area; the snoring had stopped, and she could hear a television presenter's voice instead.

She sat down and picked up her book but could not settle to read, realising with a pang that she would rather have the company of the man she had only met the previous day instead of Jared, the impossibly handsome and flawless lantern-jawed hero of her novel.

Putting the book down with a sigh, she stood up and walked painfully over to the door. She took a deep breath, shuffled out into the lobby, and knocked on his window.

"Come in!" His deep voice made her smile.

"I'm bored; how about you?" She whispered and grinned at him as she popped her head around the door.

"Bored as bored as bored can be." Alan stretched in the chair, yawned, and folded his arms. "I've even been looking at daytime TV."

"Wow; you must be desperate. It'll be lunchtime soon; I've ordered sausages and mash." Erin stood at the door, unsure whether to venture in.

"Probably the ones left over from breakfast. I don't think I can eat a thing actually, so I've only ordered some sandwiches." Alan looked up at her. "Don't just stand there, come in and keep me company!"

"Okay; I'll bring a chair from the lobby."

She turned on her heel back towards the main door of the suite. She found a small store cupboard to the right of the door and opened it, to find not only another fold-up chair, but also several jigsaw puzzles piled up behind it. Grabbing a chair and the top puzzle, she made her way back to her new friend's room.

"Look what I found as well; we can do this puzzle if you like."

Alan sat up and switched off the TV:

"I never thought I'd be so happy to see a jigsaw puzzle. Open it onto my bedside table; I'll chuck all the other stuff on the floor."

Seemingly happier, Alan cleared a space and Erin opened up the foldaway chair and brought it alongside his.

"It's a bit of a challenge, this one; a ballerina, and one thousand pieces. Shall we start with the edges first? That's what I've always done." She looked at him for confirmation.

"Yeah; I can't remember the last time I did a puzzle; Tilly must have been about four." Alan chuckled. "Let's turn all the pieces over first so that we can see what we're looking at, although I'm having trouble focusing on anything at the moment."

"Hopefully when Margaret Baines comes round she'll let us go home tomorrow and we can then start taking our thyroxine pills again." Erin whispered as she turned over some puzzle pieces, looking for straight edges.

"I'm getting desperate; my body's grinding to a halt." Alan decided to omit the fact that he was as constipated as the proverbial corncrake.

"Mine too; I'm too much of a lady to mention just how slow everything's become." Erin blushed and wished she could have retracted her last statement. She fitted two straight edges together. "That's a start, anyway."

He decided to throw caution to the wind, with the sure and certain knowledge that he could say just what he liked, as after the following day they would be more than likely be going their separate ways.

"I can't eat 'cos to be perfectly honest, nothing's coming out the other end." He picked up a corner and slotted a likely looking piece into it, grunting with satisfaction.

"Join the club; I feel like one of those clockwork mice that needs winding up. I've come to a complete halt. Food stays in my stomach for hours."

"I think I'll phone for some brown bombers or something, then you'd better stand well back while I let the cork out." Alan slotted in another piece of the jigsaw.

Erin snorted with laughter:

"I always thought that men were full of shit, and now I *know* it's true!"

"Hey, hey, we're not that bad! *Who* got out of bed and made *who* a cup of tea when they were calling for Hughie, Frank and Ralph last night?" Alan's face took on a pseudo-wounded expression.

"Yeah, I suppose so. Perhaps you're the only decent male in the whole sorry species." Erin sighed. "Have you got any bits that make up her feet over there?" She reached over and sorted through a pile of whitish puzzle pieces.

"Help yourself. I'm a decent guy. I must be a bit too decent, otherwise Tina wouldn't have run off with Doofer the Roofer." Alan succeeded in keeping his voice light and breezy. "Perhaps I should have played the field, gambled away the housekeeping, or drank myself witless every night." He handed over several white puzzle pieces absent-mindedly.

"Oh yes, we women only think we're living when we're crying over some bastard. It's why we were put upon this earth." Erin slotted in two more pieces rather forcefully.

"Ah; the entire male species has been saved by the bell." Alan stood up. "I'll get the lunches; we can put the trays on our laps."

"Okay, but when we've washed up after lunch I think I should go back into my room and wait for the physicist." Erin followed Alan's retreating back as he moved out into the lobby.

"Sure; I'll try not to complete all the puzzle while you're gone."

"You'd better not."

# CHAPTER 36

MARGARET BAINES PEERED at the readings on her Geiger counter.

"How do you feel this afternoon, Ms Mason?"

Erin had a brief mental image of Alan suffering from the possible after-effects of a brown bomber, and tried hard not to laugh.

"I've stopped feeling sick, but I'm terribly constipated."

"Ah; that's a side-effect of low thyroxine. The body grinds to a halt I'm afraid."

"When can I take my tablets again?"

"Well, the readings are coming down nicely. It looks as if you'll be able to start them tomorrow morning and then go home probably after lunch, but I'll check again tomorrow afternoon to make sure."

"Great!" Erin's voice croaked with happiness.

"Take a few more showers, but it all looks good. You can carry on with your T threes for another week, but then you'll have to swap them for the longer-acting T fours. We'll give you a week's supply of T fours, and you can order more from your GP once you get home." Margaret smiled and packed away her instruments.

"Thanks very much."

"Oh, and you'll need to come back on Friday morning for a Gamma scan. We'll need to check where in the body the radioactive iodine has been taken up."

"What time shall I come?"

"The nurse will tell you tomorrow when she completes your discharge papers."

Erin could hear Margaret knocking on Alan's window. She sat down and picked up her reading book and leafed through a few chapters until she heard the outer door to the suite close again. She gave it ten minutes before deciding whether to check if Alan wanted some company, but as soon as she stood up to go she could see his beaming moon face framed behind the open slats of her viewing window. She beckoned for him to come in.

"I can go home tomorrow! Yipee!" Alan opened the door, grinning from ear to ear.

"Yeah, me too. Looks like we won't get time to finish the puzzle now." She allowed a faint tinge of regret to pass her lips, and hoped against hope that he would pick it up.

"Who cares? I can try to get back to some semblance of a normal life again after today." Alan smiled. "Have you got to come back for a scan on Friday morning?"

"Yeah, but I don't know what time." Erin shrugged her shoulders.

"Me too; how about we meet up in the hospital canteen for lunch after our scans? I'll be able to let you know if I'm still bunged up!" Alan laughed.

"Ooh, too much information if I'm eating, thanks." Erin tried to appear nonchalant. "Yeah; I'll be around here again on Friday lunchtime. Why not?"

"Great." Alan rubbed his hands together. "They're putting two brown bombers in the hatch tonight."

"One each?" Erin felt the corners of her mouth starting to turn upwards.

"No, bugger off. They're both for me; you'll have to order your own."

Erin laughed.

"Shall we move on swiftly and continue with the puzzle?"

"Sure. Come back to my gaff then." He turned back towards the door.

She felt a strange relief knowing she could meet up with him again. He pulled up the plastic foldaway seat, and offered her the more comfortable armchair. They sat contentedly side by side and continued with the jigsaw.

"Where do you live?" Alan fitted in the last of the straight edged pieces. "That's the outside done anyway."

"On the Goldmark Estate."

"Oh yeah, I know it. I've got a mate who used to live there."

"Sounds like he saw sense and moved out. Whereabouts are you?" She started to fit the ballerina's face together; it seemed the easiest part of the puzzle to do.

"Moffatt Court, just off the Leas Road; only a few miles from your estate."

"The twins go to a youth club near there."

"Tilly probably went to it as well." Alan nodded. "I'll ask her if she remembers two ginger twin boys."

"The terrible twosome, especially Kieran; nobody usually forgets him." Erin grimaced.

"Shall I come and pick you up on Friday? I was going to ask Matty to drive me, but if I can start my T threes again tomorrow I might feel okay by then." Alan looked at her. "Were you going to drive yourself?"

"No; I was going to phone Mum later on and ask her to do it, but if you're offering I'll take you up on that. Thanks very much. My mum never stops talking shite; it does my head in."

Alan chuckled and reached up onto the bedside cabinet for his mobile phone.

"That's okay; it makes sense if we're both going to the same place. What's your address? I'll put it in my phone."

"Twenty four St. Faith's Close."

"Got it; my mate used to live around the corner from there. Have you got your phone on you? Let's swap numbers and you can let me know what time your scan will be."

Erin felt a small *frisson* of excitement surge through her as she tapped Alan's number into her contact list. She had no idea what would happen after her scan, but then again, Friday was a long way away. However, as the ballerina began to take a rough shape under her hands she realised there was one thing she did know. She smiled to herself with the secret knowledge that whatever happened after Friday, she was totally grateful to Tina Beaumont for running off with a chap called Doofer the roofer.

# CHAPTER 37

"YOU'VE WOKEN ME UP."

"Sorry; I forgot about your afternoon nap. The physicist has just been, and I've been told I can go home."

"Oh; how are you? Have I got to come out now?"

Her mother's voice sounded thin and quavery. Erin took a deep breath and jumped in before she was interrupted.

"I'm feeling a bit better today. I've taken a thyroxine tablet. You can come and get me this afternoon about four o'clock. Is that okay?" Erin's voice strained to get all the sentence out in one go.

"I always have my hair done on Wednesday afternoons."

"Well, whenever you come out of the hairdressers then; no rush."

"Okay; I think the chiropodist visits the surgery on Wednesdays too."

"Perhaps you can go next week?"

"My toe's killing me, but I'll come and get you later on then."

"Thanks. 'Bye for now."

As she quickly replaced the receiver, Erin was glad to have got her message across without having to stay on the phone too long listening to her mother's complaints. She could hear Alan and Margaret Baines talking through the party wall. She stood up, pulled down her bag from the top of the wardrobe, and started to pack up her clothes and toiletries. She felt somewhat sad to be leaving the cosy confines of their two lead-lined rooms; they had completed the ballerina puzzle together the previous evening, and then after supper had sat quite happily watching a comedy film on TV. It seemed as though she had known him all her life, and she felt quite amazed every time she remembered that she had only known him for two days.

She pushed her unread novel down on top of her clothes, and zipped up the bag. Outside in the lobby she heard Margaret come out and open the main door to the suite. Erin opened the door of her room, and laughed as Alan's face appeared around his door at the same time.

"I was just coming to knock for you." He stepped out into the lobby. "I'm clean again; I can go home. I've phoned Matty to come and get me at five o'clock when he's locked up the garage. How about you?"

Erin hid the pang of regret.

"Yeah, my mum's coming here later to talk me to death on the way home. I'm packed already. Did Margaret Baines say anything to you about not being around pregnant women and children for a couple of days, and not cooking food for anyone?"

"Yeah, something like that. She also told me not to go out any more today after I get home, and to wash all my clothes." Alan scratched his head. "I'm going to tell Matty to pick Tilly up from college and take her to his place. I don't want to take any chances."

"I'll tell Chris not to send the boys back until the weekend as well."

"Will we set the alarms off outside when we're released?" Alan looked towards the main door of the suite.

"No, not if the Geiger counter was working properly. We're clean, remember?" Erin smiled.

"Well, I'd better pack up." Alan fidgeted awkwardly.

"Sure. Don't forget to put the puzzle back in the box."

"I enjoyed doing that. God knows when I'll ever do another one." Alan turned away back to his room. "I'll knock and say goodbye when I'm packed."

"Okay."

Erin closed her door again, switched on the TV, and tried to lose herself in a mindless game show. As it drew nearer to five o'clock, she became agitated; Alan had not knocked on the door, and her mother was due at any time. Finally, she could stand it no longer; she went out into the lobby and rapped on the window.

"Hi. I was just going to knock to say goodbye." Shaved and showered, Alan opened the door dressed in a clean shirt and jeans, and with some new trainers on his feet.

"My mum will be here shortly; I thought I'd knock; see you on Friday?" Erin smiled and stood in the doorway.

"Yeah, of course. Come in."

With some dismay Erin could see that he had been watching the same moronic quiz programme. Thoughts suddenly started to run around in her brain.

*Why hadn't he come to her room a bit earlier? They had wasted an hour watching television in separate rooms when they could have been chatting!*

"All packed?" She looked around at the bare surfaces and could not for the life of her think of anything else to say.

"Yeah. Matty's just phoned to say he's locked up and he's on his way."

"Thanks for coming to my rescue that first night. You saw me at my absolute worst; sorry about that." She smiled shyly at him and was rewarded with an answering grin.

"That's okay; I've always been told I'm cool in a crisis. But thinking about it…" He hesitated and shuffled slightly from one foot to the other, "I should have seen you at your best to start with; everything was arse about tit, so to speak. Tell you what; how about if you slap on the makeup and tart yourself up tomorrow night? I'll drive over to your place. We can't go out so I'll bring a takeaway over with me if you like?"

She almost sighed with relief.

"Sounds good to me; we'll only be sitting alone at home. We might as well keep each other company again."

"Yeah, that's what I was thinking." Alan beamed from ear to ear and stopped shuffling his feet. "I'll pop over about seven o'clock then. Do you like Chinese?"

"Love it."

"See you tomorrow then."

She wanted to give him a hug, but at that moment the door to the suite opened, and he raised his arm to wave to somebody behind her. She turned to see a sturdily built young man in his early twenties acknowledge the wave.

"Hey, Matty. Cheers for coming to get me. Where's Tilly?"

"She's with Mum and Dad. I'll drop you home and then I'll bring her back after the weekend."

"Okay; this here's Erin. She's great at doing jigsaw puzzles."

"How's it going, Erin?" Matty smiled and held out a huge arm.

"A lot better now I can go home." Erin returned the smile and shook his hand.

"Nice to meet you." Matty looked over Erin's head towards Alan. "Ready?"

"Yeah; see you tomorrow, Erin."

"Bye."

Erin was quick to notice a flicker of interest pass over Matty's face before it was rapidly extinguished. She wondered how long it would take for Alan's daughter to find out that her father had arranged a date with an unknown woman for the following evening.

# CHAPTER 38

"WOW, YOU LOOK stunning, but thinking about it I'm not sure if I prefer the stripy pyjamas!"

Alan still felt rather weary, but a certain part of him was reacting furiously to the beautiful redhead standing in the doorway. He was glad of the cover of a jacket, and felt like a tongue-tied teenager.

"Come in; that Chinese smells great. I'm getting my appetite back now." Erin ushered him into the hallway.

"Cheers; so am I, but the glands in my neck feel a bit swollen today." Alan fingered his neck with one hand as he spoke, and tried to ignore his other urgent swelling, in the hope that it would eventually go away.

"My legs still ache, but the salivary glands are okay."

He looked appreciatively at Erin's legs for as long as he could get away with, and then followed her into the main living area. She had already set the table for two, and had poured out two glasses of chilled white wine.

"We'll just have to dish up out of the cartons." He opened the first carton and looked inside. "Yum; chop suey. I didn't know what you liked, so I got a bit of everything."

Erin was aware that Alan could not take his eyes off her. She had taken time and trouble with her appearance, and had been really pleased with the result.

"It all looks lovely; I've had a good sleep today and am so much better." She felt like a desirable young woman again, instead of a washed-up, middle-aged, divorced mother of two.

"Isn't it amazing what those little pills can do? I'm not shuffling about like an old man now." Alan lifted out some chop suey onto one of the plates. "Do you still feel tired?"

Erin helped herself to some prawn balls and a spring roll.

"Yeah, a bit weary I suppose, but not as bad as I was earlier in the week.  I could hardly keep my eyes open on Monday."

"You and me both." He laughed and took a rack of spare ribs. "My eyes didn't seem to be focusing properly either."

"I just thought you were short-sighted." She teased him and laughed.

"My daughter can't wait to meet you." Alan feasted his eyes on Erin and twirled some chop suey around on his fork. "She was on the phone virtually as soon as Matty got back. Whatever he said to her was definitely to your advantage."

"Oh God."

"No; Tilly's fine. She'll give you the once over, and then you'll be friends for life."

"Had she met my boys before at the youth club?" Erin savoured the non-metallic taste of a spring roll.

"I forgot to ask. Probably; she went there for years." Alan sipped some wine. "I'd better stay with just the one glass of this or I'll might nod off again."

"How's the eyes doing now?" Erin took some egg fried rice out of the container.

"You're a sight for them, that's for sure." Alan smiled. "I can focus fine now, and I like what I'm seeing." He decided to take his old Mum's advice for once and tell the truth.

Erin coloured slightly under her foundation; her heart was racing like a schoolgirl's. It had been many years since a man had made her feel desirable, and she was enjoying the experience. At that precise moment she cared not two hoots about having cancer; the man sitting opposite her was making her feel as though she was the most beautiful woman in the world. It was almost enough to turn a girl's head.

"Who could have ever thought that we'd meet the way we did? I could have had some old man of ninety next door, and so could you actually!" Erin's tinkly laugh echoed around the room.

"Yeah; I did wonder who was in the next room. I couldn't wait until the first mealtime to find out. I was hoping for at least someone to have a chat with, but you've surpassed all my expectations. I hope you're going to agree that we can carry on seeing each other." Alan finished his glass of wine and looked at her as he picked up his fork again.

"I'd like that. I don't have to put on airs and graces with you; you've seen me at my worst anyway." Erin shrugged her shoulders and tried to keep the excitement out of her voice.

"Come round and meet Tilly tomorrow after the scans. She'll be home from college about 4 o'clock."

"What's she studying?" Erin felt slightly nervous at the thought of it.

"She's doing all her secretarial exams; Business studies, Word Processing, Excel, Powerpoint and so on. She's doing okay too."

"Good for her. She'll be well qualified for a good P.A job when the time comes."

"Yeah; that's what I said. She's smart. This is her last year; she'll finish next June."

Erin had a sudden thought.

"Tell you what; when I go back to work I could keep an eye out at the hospital for secretarial vacancies for her. You never know; they might say yes." She rolled her eyes to the heavens; "That's if I ever get back to work."

"I didn't know you worked at the hospital?" Alan looked at her questioningly.

"Yes, I'm a ward clerk. But who's ever heard of a ward clerk with no voice? I'm signed off sick at the moment."

"It sounds a bit better today; you've got a croak there instead of just a whisper." He smiled as he emptied the carton of rice.

"Great; just right for answering the ward phone all day." She sighed. "Still; every cloud has a silver lining. If I hadn't had cancer I'd never have met you."

"I'd gladly have cancer for the rest of my life just so long as we can be friends." He reached one hand across the table towards her.

"Thanks for cheering me up, Alan." She laid her hand on top of his.

"It's the other way around; I feel like I've known you forever. Can I come round and pick you up tomorrow for our scans? What time is yours?"

"Half past ten." She nodded in agreement. "That would be great, thanks."

"Mine's at quarter past eleven. We can go for some lunch afterwards."

"Yeah; great. I hope it's not enclosed; I'm a bit claustrophobic. How about if I'm stuck in there and they go off for a cup of tea or something and forget about me?" She shuddered at the thought.

"It'll be fine; I'll see if I can stay in there with you."

He stood up and walked around to her side of the table and held out his arms. She rose to her feet and felt the warmth of his body as he pulled her to him.

"You've no idea how those few words have helped me." She looked up at him gratefully.

"You're welcome. I'd follow you anywhere; I don't want to lose sight of you now."

His lips brushed hers falteringly at first, but then with some eagerness on receiving her swift response. They stood locked together in their first embrace, and in the silence of their thoughts she wondered how on earth she would have ever got through the treatment without him.

# CHAPTER 39

"PLEASE COULD YOU empty your bladder and drink this glass of water to wash any radiation out of the salivary glands before climbing onto the scanner bed. We've been through your Gamma scan check list, but are there any metal objects in your pockets at all?"

Erin's heart began to race as she caught sight of the scanner. She took the glass of water and shook her head as she whispered to the young male technician.

"No metal. Is it possible that my friend could stay in here with me? He's just had his scan; he's having the same treatment as me."

"We ask for friends and relatives to wait outside. I'll be in the room with you at all times. We have a box of CD's here. If you'd like to pick one you can listen to some music during your scan. Patients often find music soothing."

She drank most of the water, riffled through the box, and picked out a Queen CD.

"I'll try to lose myself in 'Bohemian Rhapsody'."

"That makes a change. I was getting really cheesed off with U2." The technician switched on the CD player and indicated towards a small toilet off to one side.

On her return, Erin managed to smile at the technician as she climbed onto the scanner bed.

"There are camera plates above and below you. They will come quite close to your face, but will not actually touch you. They will take pictures from your head to just below your pelvis. Are you comfortable enough?" The technician made some small adjustments to the scanner as he looked at her.

"No, but just let's get it over with."

*'Is this the real life?*
*Is this just fantasy?*
*Caught in a landslide,*
*No escape from reality..........'*

Freddie Mercury's dulcet tones washed over her as she closed her eyes. She sensed the bed moving inside the camera plates, kept her eyes shut, and concentrated on the lyrics.

*'Open your eyes,*
*Look up to the skies*
*And see........'*

She did not dare open her eyes. She thought back to Alan's kiss the night before and the promise it held. She remembered the sight of him in his dressing gown at three o'clock in the morning. As light came behind her eyelids once again and the plates finally moved away from her head, she relaxed somewhat and imagined him without his dressing gown.

*'……Sent shivers down my spine,*
*Body's aching all the time….'*

Without moving a muscle she smiled inwardly.

*'……..I don't wanna die. I sometimes wish I'd never been born at all…'*

As Brian May's guitar solo moved to a crescendo, she affirmed to herself that she too was not ready to die yet either. She wanted her boys back at home, and was eager to test the waters of her new found friendship. Without undergoing the surgery, radiation and scans, she knew there would be no future. As the scanner moved down over her body she realised that she would have to endure whatever it took to be able to achieve her goals.

*'……….just gotta get out, just gotta get right out of here……..'*

She sighed and longed to be out from under the scanner's plates. As Bohemian Rhapsody changed into 'I Want to Break Free', she imagined herself wriggling out, jumping off the bed, and running into Alan's arms outside, who strangely had become the owner of a big Freddie moustache, and who now sported two balloon breasts, a pink sleeveless top, a short skirt, and black stockings with suspenders.

Finally it was done. Freddie had unknowingly helped her to endure from beyond the grave. Erin opened her eyes, sat up slowly, and smiled at the technician, who walked over to the CD player and turned it off.

"Did the music help?"

"Yeah; just a bit." She gathered her thoughts, climbed off the bed, and picked up her bag.

"The results will take a month or so to come through. You'll receive an appointment to see your oncologist in due course."

"Thanks very much."

She waved to Alan, still waiting outside. Erin smiled and imagined how he might look wearing a big Freddie Mercury moustache.

# CHAPTER 40

TILLY MISSED NOTHING as she poured tea into three mugs. Alan could see his daughter's eyes taking in every inch of Erin, as she sat rather stiffly upright on the sofa.

"So you were in the room next door to Dad at the hospital then?"

"Yes; thanks for the tea." Erin took a mug from Tilly and wondered how long the third degree interrogation would go on for.

"Have you got thyroid cancer too?"

"Yes; a bit worse than your Dad's, hence the voice problem, but treatable I think." She looked to Alan for support, who was busy stirring sugar into his tea.

"Are you divorced?" Tilly handed round a plate of biscuits.

"Don't be so nosey. Erin's come for tea, not the third degree." Alan *tutted* with annoyance as he took three custard creams.

"It's okay. Your daughter's only looking out for you. She wants to make sure who you're bringing into the house."

Erin laughed. "Ask away Matilda, I don't mind." She whispered and waved away the plate of biscuits.

"You should have seen one of the women Dad brought home once. He met her when he took me trampolining. She was divorced with six kids to feed, and guess who she wanted to help feed them?" Tilly clucked like an old mother hen and shook her head.

"She had three kids, it just seemed like six." Alan took another biscuit.

"She was *awful*, Dad."

"Well, I've only got two, and their dad pays towards their upkeep." Erin kept a fixed smile on her face as she sipped her tea. "I work at the hospital and I've got my own house."

"Sorry; I didn't mean to pry." Matilda blushed. "It's nice to meet you. Dad hasn't stopped talking about you since he came home yesterday after his scan."

"All good I hope?" Erin laughed and looked at Alan.

"Absolutely. He's been mooning about here like a teenager." Matilda chuckled.

"Tilly, will you shut up?" Alan put his empty mug down on the table, sat back in his armchair and glared at his daughter.

Erin finished her tea, relaxed slightly, and turned towards Matilda.

"When do you finish college? Are you looking for jobs yet?"

"My final exams will be next June or July. I'll start looking after Christmas I think." Matilda smiled and curled up on the floor by her father.

"I could look out for any secretarial jobs at the hospital if you like. Hopefully I'll be back at work by then."

"Yeah; that'll be great, thanks. I'm working on increasing my typing speed in the meantime. Do your sons go to the college in town?"

"Yes; Kevin's started a plumbing course, and Kieran's doing business management. They're the two red-headed identical twins."

"Oh yes, I've seen them I think; in the canteen at lunchtime." Matilda nodded.

"That'll be them; always first in the queue for food." Erin rolled her eyes to the heavens. "They eat me out of house and home. Their dad's bringing them back tomorrow. I've missed them actually." Her voice faltered and she looked down at the floor.

Matilda looked at Erin and wrapped her left arm around her father's leg possessively as she sat on the carpet next to him with her back against his armchair:

"You've got nice hair."

"Thanks. It's naturally wavy. The boys inherited it, and they absolutely detest the fact. Kieran always says no girl is going to love him because he's ginger." Erin laughed and looked up at the girl, at the same time taking in her overly-proprietorial manner. "However, he seems to be doing just fine on the girl front as far as I can see."

"Well, it wouldn't put me off, but Matty's dark anyway. We're going shopping for an engagement ring tomorrow."

"Congratulations. Your dad told me about that."

Matilda brought her right hand around to clasp her left.

"I'm cooking for Dad and Matty later on; you're welcome to stay for dinner."

"Oh no, it's okay. I need to get home to prepare the house for the boys." At that precise moment Erin thought it might be better to back off.

"You'd better stay. Tilly's bought extra now." Alan disengaged his daughter's arm and stood up. "You'd be doing us a huge favour."

Trying hard to distinguish Matilda's thoughts on the matter under her expressionless countenance, Erin gave her shoulders a slight shrug.

"Well, what can I say? Thanks very much!" She looked at Alan and smiled.

"I'll start preparing the veg then." Matilda stood up, looking at that moment to Erin the very image of her father.

"Can I help?" Erin began to follow Matilda as she made towards the kitchen.

"No thanks; guests can take it easy."

Erin smiled as Alan came to sit beside her on the settee.

"Phew!" She mopped her brow in a theatrical manner and shook her head. "I don't think she likes me."

"She'll come around. It's been her and me for so long, that's the trouble." Alan leaned over, planted a kiss on Erin's lips, and put his arm around her. "Take no notice."

"You'll have to come over and meet the boys." She returned the kiss and enjoyed the warmth of his body through his shirt.

"Oh God."

"They're not that bad; Kieran will love you, but possibly Kevin might be the same as Tilly."

"I'll bear that in mind and wear a full suit of armour." With his other hand Alan gripped an imaginary dagger and plunged it in the direction of his heart.

"I'll have a word with him first and break him in gently."

"Good idea."

# CHAPTER 41

KIERAN PILED MORE cauliflower cheese onto his plate, along with more roast potatoes.

"I want to get a Calibra when I've passed my driving test."

"Great car, but you'll pay a fortune for insurance." Alan nodded sagely towards the only twin who was saying anything.

"Will I be able to bring it round to you for a service?"

"Of course; I'll only charge you mates' rates." Alan wanted to make it quite clear from the start that he was not opening up a free shop for Erin's boys and all their teenage friends.

"Do you need any help in the garage? I'm sixteen now; I can work on Saturdays." Kieran looked at Alan hopefully.

"Well, we'll see. I have Matty working for me now."

"I could sweep up and wash the cars." Kieran persisted.

"Kieran; don't hassle Alan. He's only come for dinner, not to listen to you going on." Erin whispered and glared at her son, whilst aware of Kevin's silence.

"Actually I *could* do with a car washer on Saturday mornings, Kieran. We only work until one o'clock though." Alan was relieved to find out at last which twin he was speaking to.

"Great! Can I start next week then?" Kieran chewed happily while he spoke.

"Er…sure. Why not?" Alan looked across at Kevin, who lowered his eyes towards his plate.

"Sorry, Alan. Kieran's got such a cheek." Erin passed him a tea towel, opened the dishwasher, and shook her head to emphasise her point.

"No, it's okay. I can afford to pay him a bit. It's your other son I'm worried about; he didn't say a single word throughout the whole of the meal and then he ran up to his room."

"I know; he's like Tilly I suppose. He's been looking after me recently and I suppose he's feeling a bit pushed out. I'll see if I can find out later on what the problem is." Erin dried some cutlery from the dishwasher and put it away. "Thanks for taking Kieran on though; send him back home if he's a pain in the arse."

"I'm sure he'll be fine." Alan finished drying the last of the crockery, put the tea towel down on the worktop, and came over to stand next to her. "Thanks so much for dinner; come here and have a cuddle."

She needed no second invitation; the welcome feel of his arms made it easy to block out reality. She lifted her face for a kiss and touched his tongue with her own.

"I've fallen for you in a big way, Erin. I just can't help it." Alan sighed and clasped both arms around her as tightly as he could.

"Me too; I can't believe this is happening so fast." She whispered and ran her fingertips up and down his back.

"Here we are, two of the unhealthiest people in the whole wide world; we were made for each other!"

Ignoring the hardness in his groin, he pressed her to him.

"We're going to cycle round and stay with Dad tonight. I've just phoned him, and he says it's okay."

Jumping away guiltily from Alan's embrace, Erin saw with some dismay that Kevin was standing in the kitchen doorway with a bulging rucksack on his back, and behind him Kieran was trying to make himself invisible, but grinning at her in the passageway.

"Oh? You've only just come home! Why are you going back?"

"Well, it's obvious to me that you don't need us around." Kevin's expression was grim, and his manner aloof.

"Kevin, that's a silly thing to say! Of course I want you around!" Erin ran over to her son. "But try and be happy for me; I've met a lovely man here." She indicated a hand towards Alan. "He's got no intention of ever taking the place of your father, but at the moment he's a good friend who's helping me through my treatment."

"I can help you through your treatment." Kevin gazed down at the floor, close to tears.

Erin's heart went out to her son. She put her hands on his shoulders, but the boy flinched and pulled away.

"Yes I know you can; you cooked me some lovely meals before I had to go into hospital and I'm very grateful, but you two are growing up and pretty soon you'll be off into the world doing your own thing. I also need to make a life for myself. I've met Alan and I want him around now, but it doesn't change how I feel about the pair of you."

"Would you like to work with your brother at my garage on Saturday mornings?" Alan desperately tried to make amends.

"No thanks." Kevin looked at his shoes. "We'll be back tomorrow morning, Mum. Dad's asked Kieran to come over as well."

"See you in the morning, Mum. 'Bye Alan!" Kieran waved cheerily from the passageway.

As the front door slammed, Erin fell back tearfully into Alan's arms.

"Nobody said it would be easy." Alan patted her back. "We've both alienated our children, so there's only one thing for it now."

"What?"

"We've got the house to ourselves. Let's see how I can help you make a life for yourself tonight." He kissed her and held her close.

"You'd better do it soon then; I don't know about yours, but my thyroxine levels peter out every evening around half past eight." Erin smiled and ran her finger along the still-visible scar on his neck. "Let's go upstairs."

She allowed him to undress her slowly. When she was naked she sat down on the bed in front of him and watched with a growing arousal as he removed his clothes. His penis was already erect, and she gripped the backs of his thighs and ran her tongue along its length.

"Ah; stop that for a minute. It's been a long while; I'll come too soon."

His head was tipped backwards and his eyes were closed. Erin lay back on the pillows and giggled as he came back to reality, and climbed over her supine form to join her on the bed.

"You're hairy like a werewolf!" She propped herself up in bed on one elbow to look at him in the lamplight, and giggled.

"Bloody cheek, I'm not that bad! Your body is like strawberries and cream though." Alan turned to her and ran one hand over her breasts. "I've never seen anything so beautiful."

He moved on top of her and took one of her nipples in his mouth. Erin groaned, closed her eyes and arched her back, and not for the first time wondered how the hell she could have gone from abject misery to utter elation in the space of one short week. She opened her legs to him and felt his tongue move up and down her engorged clitoris.

"That feels so good."

Her broken voice was thick with emotion as she gripped her knees in order to spread her thighs wider. When her climax came she curled her upper body and shuddered as his tongue licked further inside her vagina. The sensation was almost overpowering.

"Nobody's ever done that to me before." Spent, she flopped back onto the pillows.

"It's just kinky the first time." He whispered in her ear as he moved back on top.

When she felt him enter her she wrapped her legs around his back and drew him into the wetness of her core. They moved together quickly in a rhythm of their own, each lost in the wonder of the other. When she felt his release she clenched and released the muscles of her perineum to add to his pleasure.

"I love you Erin; now I've found you I'll never let you go." He kissed her deeply, further excited by her response.

"I love you too. I'm not going anywhere without you." She felt the sated, limp weight of him on her and smiled.

# CHAPTER 42

"MS MASON AND ER…..Mr Beaumont?"     Doctor Ingram looked down and checked his notes.

"Yeah; we want to be seen together." Alan held Erin's hand and nodded.

"I see. Well………who's first?"

"Ladies first." Alan indicated towards Erin with a free thumb.

"Okay. Ms Mason; how is your scar? Healing well?"

"Yes thanks. No problems there."

"Good. We have the results back from your Gamma scan. It shows there was uptake of radioiodine in the neck area around the thyroid bed only. However, because of this and your still-raised thyroglobulin level in your recent blood test, this tells us that the cancer is still present. Fortunately though, as far as I am aware, it has not spread to other parts of the body. Therefore you will still need another dose of radioactive iodine in about five months' time to kill off any remaining cancer cells."

"Oh no, not again!" Erin's world came crashing down for a second time. She gripped Alan's hand harder and fought to stop tears forming behind her eyes.

"For a second dose however, it is not necessary to stop your thyroxine medication beforehand. With two intramuscular injections of thyrogen a few days beforehand, you can carry on as normal. A district nurse from your GP surgery will visit you at home and administer the injections. Patients do not normally experience as many side-effects with a second injection, as there are less cancer cells present for the radioiodine to cling to."

Erin wanted to burst into tears at the thought of it.

"At least you won't need to stop taking your thyroxine." Alan gave her hand a squeeze.

"Oh God, I've got to go through it all again though!" Erin sighed.

"One more dose should be enough. How do you feel on your new T4 tablets?" Doctor Ingram looked at Erin. "Any palpitations, hot flushes or rapid heartbeats?"

"I often feel hot, and my heart seems to be beating faster a lot of the time" Erin suddenly wondered whether it was due to the tablets or Alan's constant nearness.

"Are you still taking the one hundred and seventy five microgram dose?" Doctor Ingram checked his notes again.

"Yes, but if I bend forward I can hear my heart pounding in my ears. Am I on too much?" Erin looked at the oncologist questioningly.

"It would appear so. Reduce to one hundred and fifty micrograms per day and see how you feel on that, and have another blood test in eight weeks. We have to make sure you are not too over-medicated, as too much thyroxine in your system could also cause bone thinning in the future and weight loss, as well as the heat and palpitations you are feeling now. We will book you for a bone scan in due course, and I'll see you again for a follow up in two months' time before your next radioiodine treatment and after your repeat blood test to check your new thyroxine levels."

"Great; it just gets better and better, doesn't it?" Erin looked at Alan and sighed again.

"Have you had your vocal cords checked by the ENT department yet? As your cancer was rather advanced, the surgeon will be able to see if there has been any damage to the nerve by manipulation during your thyroidectomy."

"I'm still waiting for an appointment, but Mr Barker-Lomax told me my voice would come back." Erin's whisper held a note of panic.

"It should, and many patients see improvement after about six months, but an ENT specialist will be able to help you further if there has been any permanent damage."

"How can they call this a 'good' cancer?" Erin shook her head.

She could not see any light at the end of the tunnel. She put her head on Alan's shoulder, who put an arm around her and let her weep bitter tears.

Dr Ingram coughed and looked up from his notes.

"Mr Beaumont; how are you today?"

"I'm fine; still a bit tired sometimes, but feeling better on the two hundred microgram dose." Alan kissed the top of Erin's forehead and looked back up at the specialist.

"How is your scar?"

"Healing okay. No problems." Alan reached over and passed Erin a tissue from a box on the doctor's desk.

"There has been no uptake of radioiodine on your scan, so you will not need a second dose. We will continue to monitor you with blood tests and sometimes CT or MRI scans, but for now you need no further treatment other than to continue with your thyroxine medication. I'll make an appointment for you to be followed up in three months' time with a repeat blood test and an MRI scan of your head, neck and chest with contrast. We don't like giving too many CT scans, due to the amount of radiation present in each one."

"Great; thanks doc." Alan cuddled Erin and almost felt guilty for getting away so lightly.

"I now need to check both your necks, so could I have Ms Mason first on the examination chair please."

Erin stood up shakily, wiped her eyes, and walked over towards the oncologist. As she felt his fingers probing down around her windpipe area she wanted to swat him away like an irritating fly.

"Your neck feels fine; nothing untoward there. You can sit back in your seat."

She changed places with Alan, who shot her a supporting smile.

"No problems, Mr Beaumont. I can't feel any lumps in your neck either."

As they left the consultation room Erin managed to hold off any more tears until they arrived back at the multi-storey. However, as she flopped down in the passenger seat of Alan's car, her whole life flashed before her. She threw her arms around his neck, buried her face in his shoulder, and howled like a helpless baby.

# CHAPTER 43

"WE SEEM TO have Saturday mornings to ourselves now." Erin smiled at Kevin over the breakfast table.

"Yeah." Kevin chewed his bacon roll thoughtfully.

"Is everything okay? You've been very quiet lately." She spread some margarine noisily on a piece of toast.

"I'm alright."

"Can I ask you something?"

"What?" He looked up at her.

"How do you feel about me and Alan?" She held her breath as she waited for a response.

"What does it matter? You'll carry on seeing him whatever I say." Kevin shrugged and carried on eating.

"We're all entitled to find happiness in this world. I loved your father, but he loved somebody else. I've been given a second chance; he makes me happy, Kevin." She exhaled slowly.

"Fair enough."

"What is it about him that you don't like? It's important for me to know." She put down her toast and looked at her son.

"He's always round here. I don't like meeting him on the landing in the mornings in his dressing gown." Kevin added more tomato sauce to his bacon.

"His daughter is older than you and Kieran, and she's recently moved out to live with her fiancée. Alan's on his own now. I like living here with you two, and don't want to leave you on your own every weekend while I stay over at his place. It makes sense for him to come here."

"Whatever." Kevin shrugged again and carried on chewing.

Erin felt at her wit's end.

"So it's not Alan himself you don't like, it's the fact that he stays here sometimes?"

"I don't like him or the fact that he stays here; he's slimy." Kevin wrinkled his nose.

"Slimy?"

"Yeah. Slimy and slithery like a fat snake." Kevin picked up a cup of tea.

"Kevin, that's unfair. He's nothing of the kind." Erin looked across the table. "What about Marie?"

"What about her?"

"Do you speak to her, or do you ignore her as well?" "I speak to her if I have to." "So you don't like her either?"

"Not much." Kevin placed his cup down on the table and put his head in his hands.

"Hey, what's wrong?" Erin moved around to Kevin's side of the table and put an arm around his shoulders.

"It used to be you, Dad, Kieran and me. Then Dad went off with Marie, and now you're off with Alan." Kevin's face crumpled. "Why can't you get back with Dad?"

"Dad's with Marie, and I've found Alan, but it doesn't mean that we don't love you and Kieran just the same as we always did. Do you want me to be lonely and miserable for the rest of my life?" Erin gave him a squeeze.

"You won't be lonely; you've got me." Kevin sniffed and ran a hand across his eyes.

"And I'm glad I've got you, but one day the pair of you will both find girls to love who will make you happy and content. I've been on my own for a long time, but Alan's made such a difference to my life in just a few months. You haven't had time to get used to him yet. Give him a chance and he'll grow on you."

"Yeah, like a fungus." Kevin managed a weak grin.

Erin wracked her brain and tried one last tack.

"When I have to go back into hospital for some more radiation Alan's volunteered to stay here and make sure the two of you are okay."

"We don't need any babysitter."

"He won't talk all the time like Nan does."

"He never talks to me at all if I'm in the same room as him." Kevin lifted his head up from his hands and looked at her.

"That's because you're giving him such a hard time. He doesn't know what to do." Erin sighed.

"I'm sorry Mum, I just want it to be how it used to be." Kevin sat back in his chair and looked down at the table.

"Things change, and we have to do away with the old and accept the new. Please promise me that you'll try and give Alan a chance?"

"I'll try." He looked at her. "Are you going to die?" "Not for a long time yet, Kev. I've got cancer but it's treatable. Alan's in remission now, but I just need one more dose of radiation."

"Love you, Mum." He threw his arms around her neck. "I'm sorry."

"It's okay." She patted his back like she had done so many years ago. "It's okay."

# CHAPTER 44

"COME IN MS MASON!"

Erin thought she could possibly win any competition that was to do with collecting a certain amount of doctors in one year. She sighed and held out her right hand.

"Nice to meet you, Mr Hughes."

The ENT surgeon waved her towards an empty chair.

"Come and sit down and tell me about your voice."

Erin looked at the young consultant and liked the look of him almost immediately.

"I've only got a few tones in the lower register, and a kind of two-tone breathy whisper in the upper regions. It's only got a tiny bit better since my thyroidectomy just over three months' ago. I'm still on sick leave from work due to having no voice."

Mr Hughes nodded sagely.

"If the vocal cord has been damaged by manipulation during surgery it could take six to nine months for you to see any improvement. For now, if you are agreeable, I'll give you some anaesthetic spray through your nose which will numb the back of your throat, and I'll then be able to have a look at your vocal cords with my camera."

Her heart started beating faster with nerves at the prospect, but she was not one to take the easy option.

"Okay."

She found the experience most disagreeable. The surgeon threaded the camera down the back of her throat slowly and carefully, as she tried to keep still while closing her eyes and thinking about Alan's naked body.

"Say eeee……"

"Eeeeee…." The sound coming from the back of her throat sounded most peculiar.

"Count from one to ten for me, please."

When the camera slid out of her nose she tried to swallow against the numbness, and tasted the anaesthetic at the back of her throat. She hoped she was not going to gag.

"Your left vocal cord is paralysed, Ms Mason. It was obviously damaged during surgery. From your notes it looks as if the surgeon had difficulty removing some lymph glands. However, as I said, we'll do nothing for now because if the nerve is only damaged it may heal with time, or if it is severed in my experience the right vocal cord will probably move over to compensate. If this does not happen then there is an operation we can do at some point in the future to strengthen your voice, but we will see what happens. I'll see you again in nine months' time."

Back at home, Erin wondered if she would ever be able to work again. While the house was quiet she sent an email to her ward manager, letting her know the result of her appointment with the ENT surgeon. She felt quite well in herself, but knew she would never be able to do her job in her present voiceless state. She received a reply almost immediately.

*'Come in and see me this afternoon if you want to come back to work. I'll have a word with HR and see if we can re-deploy you elsewhere in the hospital.'*

She felt able to do some kind of work, but only the sort that did not involve too much talking or answering the phone. Erin made herself a light lunch, sent a text to the boys to say that she may be late, and then set out for the hospital.

It felt strange going back into Somerset ward after so long away. The stench of the farmyard was still in the air as she walked through the main doors and knocked on the ward manager's office.

"Come in!"

"Hi Lisa!" Erin whispered as brightly as she could.

"Hello Erin; poor you. You've really been through the mill haven't you?" Lisa Monroe pulled up an empty chair. "Have a seat."

"Thanks." Erin sat down and wondered what was coming next.

"I've had a word with HR for you. If you're feeling well there's several alternatives. There's jobs going in the kitchen, in X-Ray, or there's a secretarial assistant post in Pain Medicine if you can type."

"I can type, but the secretaries have to answer the phones don't they?" Erin looked questioningly at Lisa.

"Not the secretarial assistants. You'll just have to type the clinic letters, that's all."

"I don't fancy kitchen work. I think I'll give the secretarial assistant post a go if that's okay?" Erin declined to point out the fact that it was a grade higher, which would obviously mean an increased in pay.

"Fine; it'll be a shame to lose you, but if you want to work then this would be the job for you at the moment. You can always come back to us if your voice returns and you'd rather be here."

Erin could think of no reason why she would want to go back down to a grade two. Sometimes there was a silver lining in the proverbial black cloud.

"Thanks Lisa; thanks very much. I'm still having treatment, but I can work in-between times if I feel well. I'll contact Pain for a start date then?"

"No; contact Muriel Cartwright, the manager of all the secretaries. She'll sort you out."

# CHAPTER 45

SHE WAS RATHER glad she did not have *symphysis pubis dystocia*, and she silently gave thanks to Google as she checked the spelling. Erin knew she was slower than the other secretaries, and wondered if they looked down on her as she grappled with unfamiliar medical terminology. As far as she could tell, she seemed to have the better job even though the secretaries were a grade higher in the salary stakes. Their phones rang incessantly while they tried to type their clinic letters, and they seemed to always be on the verge of sinking under a mountain of admin.

*What the hell was the sternocleidomastoid?*

She sighed and wrote it down in her notebook for future reference. The little book was rapidly filling up with names of drugs, diseases, and parts of the body she had never even heard of. Her head was usually spinning by the end of the day, and she looked forward to Alan's visits in the evening for some down time. As Christmas approached however, she found the doctors' dictation coming at her through the headphones was a little easier to understand, her relationship with Alan was more than comfortable, and that to her surprise she felt chilled and relaxed.

"I've been doing up an old Ford Fiesta in the garage in my spare time. It's taxed and insured in my name, and it's a good little first car. Would the boys like to share it for a Christmas present? They'll want to start learning to drive sometime in the New Year I expect, and I can add them on to my insurance when the time comes." Alan muted the TV while the adverts were showing for whiskey, mince pies and Rennies, and waited for Erin's reply.

"They're not seventeen until June. Oh God, Kieran behind the wheel of a car frightens me." Erin exhaled forcefully in his arms and shook her head.

"It'll happen sooner or later. I can take them out on the industrial estate where the garage is. There's no cars on the road after six o'clock around there."

"I'm sure they'll love it. I'm just a bit scared." Erin grimaced.

"It'll be a way for me to break the ice with Kevin. Kieran thinks the car belongs to a customer, but he'll be chuffed when he finds out it's his."

"Tell them about it at Christmas, but obviously they'll have to wait until they're seventeen."

"Sure. I'll get it finished ready for Christmas Day."

"Is there enough time left?"

"I'll stay late after Matty's gone home next week and do it."

She yawned.

"What shall we do about Christmas? Chris usually has the boys on Boxing Day. What about Tilly and Matty?"

"They're going to his parents on Boxing Day, so shall we do a combined Christmas Day at my place? We can all chip in with the cooking, and I'll get Matty to park the car in the road behind our back fence on Christmas morning; Kieran won't see it straight away then." Alan looked at her questioningly.

"It sounds great. Yes." Erin nodded. "I always get miserable at Christmas thinking of times past, so this year will be a bit different. Perhaps I'll be miserable thinking about my next treatment instead."

"You won't be miserable at all. I won't let you." Alan leaned down and gave her a kiss.

"I've never been so happy actually. I think I must be the happiest lady with advanced cancer in the whole world. Not only have I found you, I've also found a job I can do which is paying me more money!"

"Cancer brought us together. How weird is that?" Alan shook his head at the quirk of fate. "We only live a few miles apart as well. Now I can't imagine my life without you."

"I think they call it Kismet." Erin laughed. "We were made for each other."

Christmas Day dawned bright and clear. Erin woke up early and checked her phone. There was already a message from Alan wishing her a merry Christmas, and downstairs she could hear the rumble of boys' voices in the sitting room. She wrapped a robe around her, found her slippers, and went downstairs.

"Can we open our presents now? We've been waiting ages for you to come down." Kevin smiled at her as she walked towards the Christmas tree.

"Let's get to it then!" She suddenly remembered their excited faces all those years ago, and Chris sitting by the tree handing out parcels to unwrap.

She blanked out the memory and picked up the first present in the pile.

"I see this is from you, Kevin." "Hope you like it!"

She smiled at her son as she tore off the wrapping.

"What a pretty necklace! Thank you!" She held up the silver pendant and examined it.

"I thought it'd be a way for you to cover up the scar." Kevin stood up. "Can I put it on for you?"

"Of course; how thoughtful of you! I'll certainly keep it on today."

The next parcel seemed to be done up with what she recognised as duct tape.

"Sorry Mum; the shop had run out of Sellotape, so Alan lent me some of his." Kieran shrugged.

"That's okay, it's just a bit difficult to open."

She finally managed to prise a pair of silver earrings from the sticky duct tape that matched the pendant.

"Thanks so much boys! I'm certainly a lucky lady today. Open the ones from me, and then I can make a cup of tea while you open all the rest."

She had spent the last of her savings on two iPads, but the look on her sons' faces had made the sacrifice worthwhile.

"Wow! Thanks Mum!" Kevin rushed up and nearly bowled her over in his enthusiasm.

"Hey! Steady on! Glad you like it!" Erin laughed. "You're the best!" Kieran enveloped her in a bear hug and spun her around.

"Put me down!"

Laughing, she enjoyed the sight of the boys looking excitedly at their iPads:

"Don't forget we're going to Alan's for dinner. He's got a special present for you, and you'll get to meet his daughter and her fiancée today."

"We've already met at college. She came up and introduced herself in the canteen." Kieran shrugged again and turned back to his iPad.

"Have we got to go?" Kevin wrinkled his nose.

"Yes; they're putting on a dinner for us. Don't forget what I told you about making an effort."

"Okay Mum." Kevin sighed.

# CHAPTER 46

"HI BOYS; HELLO Erin. Come in; Dad's in the kitchen carving up the turkey." Tilly smiled as she opened the front door.

"Happy Christmas, Tilly. Thanks for inviting us." Erin gave Tilly a quick hug. "Would you like to put these under the tree for later?" She handed over three small parcels.

"Great; thanks. We always normally open our presents in the evening after tea."

"Actually that's not a bad idea." Erin nodded. "It gives you something to look forward to. In our house the presents are all opened first thing in the morning and it's all over by breakfast time." She chuckled and followed the boys into the kitchen.

"Hey boys! Hi Erin!" Alan looked up from a steaming roasted turkey and waved a long, thin knife in the air.

"How's it going?" Kieran sidled over to the serving platter and popped a piece of hot turkey breast into his mouth.

"Help yourself, don't stand on ceremony." Alan pulled a face at Kieran. "Piece of turkey Kevin?"

"Nah, it's okay thanks." Kevin stood awkwardly by the kitchen door.

"Can I do anything to help?" Erin gave Kevin a nudge.

"I think Tilly and I have everything under control. Matty will be here in a minute with your present, boys. We normally open them all tonight, but your one from me needs to be opened during the day."

"Why?" Kieran took another piece of turkey.

"You'll realise why when you see it."

"Can we open it before dinner?" Kevin's face registered a faint interest.

"Sure. All the veggies are cooking nicely. I'll just check where Matty is and then you can have a look." Alan tapped a message into his phone, which was answered almost immediately:

"Follow me, boys. It's out here."

Alan ushered the twins through the back door and then winked at Erin and Tilly, who trailed after him out into the garden:

"Where is it?" Kieran looked around the patio and shrugged.

"Go through that gate down there on the end wall."

Alan pointed to an exit partly obscured by evergreen shrubs. Erin, watching him smile with pleasure as he ran down the garden path to keep up with the boys, realised just at that moment how strong her feelings were for him.

"Hi!" Kieran waved as he saw Matthew climbing out of the Ford Fiesta. "I didn't know this was your car."

"It's not." Matty smiled.

"Oh? Whose is it then?"

Kieran's confused look caused Alan to burst out laughing.

"It's yours, Divbo; yours and your brother's. I've been doing it up for the pair of you. Happy Christmas!"

"Wow! Thanks!" Stunned for a moment, Kieran then looked excitedly at Kevin and ran over to grab Alan in a bear hug. "I've seen that car for weeks in the garage!"

"Yeah, it goes like a dream now. Wait until you're seventeen, and then you'll find out." Alan chuckled, returned the hug, and then looked at Kevin.

"Cheers, Alan; I wasn't expecting this." Kevin's face broadened into a grin. "Can I sit in the driver's seat?"

"As long as you don't turn the engine on. I'll get Matty to take it back to the garage later. You've only got a few more months to wait."

Erin heaved a sigh of relief, enjoying the obvious male camaraderie going on between Matty, Alan, and her sons. She noticed that Kevin had forgotten to scowl, and was grinning from ear to ear as he sat in the driver's seat.

"My turn now, turd." Kevin nudged his brother into the passenger seat with the force of his body.

"We'll have to draw up a rota for who drives it on what night." Kieran put his hands on the steering wheel and moved it slightly from side to side.

"I'll drive it every night and you can beg." Kevin punched his brother's shoulder.

"Dream on; you can pay me fifty quid every time you need to ask me for the car keys." Kieran pushed a button to open the bonnet, and got out of the car. "What's where, Alan?" He came around the front of the car.

Alan lifted up the bonnet.

"I thought I was through being a grease monkey for the day."

"Not yet." Kieran peered with interest under the bonnet.

Erin smiled at Matilda, who stood beside her:

"Come on; shall we go in and dish up? It's freezing out here."

"Good idea; I can't work out what's so interesting under the bonnet of a car. As long as it gets me from A to B I don't care." Matilda shrugged and folded her arms tightly across her chest against the chill.

"We haven't got enough testosterone, that's the problem." Erin laughed.

"Thank God for that." Matilda turned on her heel and walked back through the gate.

# CHAPTER 47

"I CAN'T TELL which one's which, now they're both talking to me." Alan chuckled and pulled Erin over to him in the bed.

"Kevin's the one talking to you through gritted teeth I expect." She laughed and slid an arm across his stomach.

"I just call both of them 'twin' now. They seem to have accepted it. Did you ever have a quiet word with Kevin then?" Alan turned towards her.

"We had a little heart to heart a while back when you and Kieran were at the garage one Saturday morning, and of course the car you gave them yesterday helped even further. Thanks so much for the dinner, and for making their day, and thanks for my perfume. That one must have cost you a fortune."

"No worries; you're worth it, and the shirt you bought me fits perfectly."

"I thought it might. I had a nosey round the last time I was over yours, and found an old one to check the collar size."

Alan chuckled.

"I'm intrigued; what sort of response did you get from Kevin when you had your heart to heart?"

"The gist of it is that he wanted his Mum and Dad to get back together again, but I think he's slowly come to realise that it's not going to happen."

"Nasty old Alan's in the way of his dream." Alan sighed and ruffled her hair. "I can't blame the poor sod. I felt the same way towards my brother-in-law when my older sister left home to get married. She'd always taken me about with her, and I felt abandoned and blamed him for years. Poor Rick; it wasn't his fault."

"You can't put old heads on young shoulders. If only we could." Erin sighed. "I think he's also frightened that I'm going to die."

"You'd better not; I've only just found you!" Alan kissed the top of her head. "I'd better look after you then and make sure you stay alive and don't run off with the handsome hunk in the room next door when you have your next dose of radiation."

Erin enjoyed the feel of his warm body next to hers and closed her eyes.

"One handsome hunk's enough for me. By the way, how is Tilly now when my name comes up in the conversation? She seemed okay yesterday."

"She's too busy with her own love life to worry about mine. Anyway, she's accepted you I think. They're talking about getting married in August when she's finished her exams."

"Wow!" Erin sat up in bed and looked at him. "Really?"

"Yeah. Matty loves her, so who am I to put up any barriers? They've got their little studio flat. They're as happy as a pig in shit." He chuckled again. "He's a good lad; hard-working too. Tilly could have done a lot worse."

Erin lay down again and wriggled on top of Alan's naked body to enjoy the closeness:

"Another appointment came through the other day for the radiation treatment at the end of February."

"You didn't tell me." His arms came over her back a little tighter.

"I had to get my head around it first."

"I'll be there every day at visiting time, don't you worry."

"It won't do you any good; you'd best stay away. You've already had one lot."

"I don't care. You won't get rid of me that easily. Besides, I'll need to check out the handsome hunk next door."

"To see what he's got that you haven't?" Erin rubbed her nose in the warm, hairy place in the centre of his chest.

"Yeah; he might have a twelve inch willie for all you know."

"Ouch. Perhaps I'll ask him how long it is if it'll put your mind at rest, and then you can see if you measure up." She kept a straight face as she lifted her head to look at him.

"Bugger off. You keep in your room, and let him and his twelve inch willie stay in his." Alan kissed the top of her head.

"What about mealtimes?" Erin tried hard not to laugh. "Perhaps I'll stick my fork in it if he comes too near the hatch."

"Yeah; pretend it's a sausage under the grill."

Alan ran his hands up and down her back.

"I'll stay at yours if you like, and keep an eye on the boys overnight while you're gone."

"You don't have to do that." Erin shook her head slightly. "I'll ask Mum, or they could stay with Chris."

"No; it's fine. Kevin's talking to me now; I'm pleased I'm making some sort of headway with him. When I give them some lessons in the car it'll crack the ice even further I hope."

"I'll ask them what they want to do. I haven't even told them about the appointment yet." Erin closed her eyes again and enjoyed the sensation of his fingers. "Actually I can hear them talking downstairs. I'd better get up, cook some breakfast, and speak to them about it."

She wriggled off him and climbed out of bed. Alan looked appreciatively at her nakedness.

"Fancy some Sunday afternoon delight when the boys go and see their dad today?"

"You're on. It'll take my mind off what I've got coming." She pulled back the duvet to gaze at his erect penis.

"It's not twelve inches, but it's serviceable."

"Yeah, it's serviceable all right." She chuckled as she put on some pyjamas. "You've got no worries there."

Padding downstairs in her bare feet she ran a hand through her hair and opened the kitchen door.

"'Morning boys; Boxing Day bacon, eggs and baked beans?" She whispered as she yawned and switched on the kettle.

"Does the Pope wear a dress?" Kieran caught some toast as it popped out of the toaster.

"Yes please, Mum." Kevin smiled.

"Had a good Christmas so far? She smiled at their young, fresh faces.

"The best; wait until we tell our mates at college that we've got a car!" Kieran held up his hand to Kevin for a high five.

"And we've got iPads!" Kevin returned the high five.

"And we haven't even opened Dad's presents yet!" Kieran's excited voice became louder.

Feeling happy in her sons' excitement, Erin decided not to spoil their happiness. *Her appointment for treatment was not until February. There was plenty of time to tell them about it.*

# CHAPTER 48

"I LEFT YOUR other present until the boys were out." Erin sat up in bed.

"Another one?  You've spent enough already!"

Alan reached over onto the floor and took a small box out of his trouser pocket.

"Open this one, and tell me what you think."

With a rapidly beating heart Erin took the box from his hands. It was a strange shape; flat and rectangular. She opened the lid to find a small Yale key hidden beneath tufts of cotton wool.

"What's this key for?" She took it out of the box and twirled it around in her fingers.

"It's the key to my house, or rather it's your key to my house…..well, what I'm trying to say is that my house is your house so to speak." Alan sighed and shook his head. "Shit. What I'm trying to say is to ask if you and the boys would like to move in with me? The house is paid for and is big enough for all of us, and now Tilly's moved out it's even bigger. There's four bedrooms, three of them are empty. I can't think of anybody else I'd rather share my life with. I love you so much, Erin. You're the one I've been waiting for all these years."

She looked at him open-mouthed and speechless for a few seconds.

"Say something then, for Christ's sake!" Alan's eyes were pleading as they scrutinised her face.

"What a lovely Christmas present! I love you too….yes!"


Erin threw her arms around his neck and kissed him soundly on the lips. They fell back against the pillows.

"Do you think the boys will be pleased? With his interest in cars I seem to be on Kieran's wavelength, and even Kevin's talking to me now." Alan smiled. "I haven't slept for days thinking of how to ask you. I know we've only known each other a few months, but I'm absolutely crazy about you."

His arms encircled her back as they lay entwined facing each other. Erin enjoyed the long-forgotten sensation of feeling safe inside a man's embrace.

"I can't believe what's happened." She looked up at him. "If we hadn't both had cancer I'd never have met you." Erin shook her head in wonder.

"What do you think the boys will say?" Alan's voice held a hint of nervousness.

"Don't worry; they're young and adaptable. They'll love having a bedroom to themselves. As you know, we've only got two, as I had to downsize after the divorce."

He moved back and held her at arm's length, taking in every inch of her naked body.

"God; you're beautiful. I'm the luckiest man alive."

He kissed her tenderly, and then with some urgency, opening her mouth with his lips and finding her tongue with his own. Excited and aroused as she lifted her head and moved on top of him, he held onto her buttocks with both hands and took one of her soft breasts into his mouth, gently teasing the nipple with his tongue.

"Ah; that feels so good." Erin whispered as she sat up and arched her back.

He propped himself up slightly and moved her buttocks apart with his hands as she eased herself onto his penis, groaning with pleasure as she straddled him and felt its hardness inside her. Moving rhythmically back and forth, she looked into his eyes and saw his own mounting excitement. Aware of when he was not able to hold out for much longer, she clenched her muscles around his penis, increased the tension on her spread legs, and allowed his final thrust to fuel her own sweet, shuddering release.

"Sweet Jesus." He closed his eyes and pulled her limp body towards him.

His heart was thudding against her ear, and she wanted the moment to last forever. She contracted her muscles again, but his hardness had dissipated somewhat.

"Stay here tonight; the boys won't be back until tomorrow. We can tell them then." She moved her hands up around his shoulders.

"I never want to spend another night apart from you ever again." Sated, Alan held her close and pulled the bedclothes up around them.

She realised that she must have dozed off on his chest. When she woke up he gave her a little squeeze.

"Was I snoring?" She hoped against hope that his answer would be in the negative.

"Like the proverbial trooper."

"Shit; sorry about that." She rolled off him.

"Don't go; I was enjoying it."

"What? The snoring?"

"No; you laying on top of me."

"Cuddle up to my back then."

She turned onto her side, closed her eyes, and knew no more until the morning.

# CHAPTER 49

LOOKING DOWN THE passage, Erin could see two squashed noses and two familiar red heads pressed up against the smoked glass of the front door. She whispered to Alan as he sat at the kitchen table reading a newspaper.

"Can you let the boys in please? I've got my hands in pastry."

"Sure."

Leaving the newspaper open, he smiled at her and wandered off down the hallway. As he opened the door she looked up from her mixing bowl and was surprised to see Chris standing behind the boys.

"Hi Mum!" The twins' voices shouted in unison as they dumped their bags down and raced each other up the stairs to their room.

Erin quickly washed her hands, aware of the awkward silence in the hallway.

"Hi boys! Hi Chris, everything okay?" She wiped her hands on her apron as she came to stand next to Alan.

"Er……..yeah.  I just wanted a word if that's okay with you?" Chris, large and solid, stood ill-at-ease on the doorstep, ignoring Alan.

"Come in then."

"I'll carry on reading the paper." Alan shrugged and turned to go back towards the kitchen.

Chris walked in the opposite direction towards the front room, and closed the door as she followed in behind him. She watched with some irritation as he took a seat in his old armchair and made himself at home.

"What's up?"

He stretched out his long legs and looked down at the carpet.

"He's bought my sons a car."

"So?"  Her irritation started to grow.

"So ….. what's he trying to do?  They're not even seventeen yet."

"He knows that. He's keeping it for them at his garage until they can learn to drive."

"It should be me buying them a car. You know I can't afford to do that."

"That's because you left them and ran off with somebody else. You're keeping two families now; it's hard on the bank balance." Her anger began to bubble away like the magma beneath the surface of an erupting volcano.

She watched the muscles in his jaw tense and relax.

"So he's got his feet under the table now then?" He looked up at her and crossed his legs.

"Yes he has, and as soon as you're gone I'm going to tell the boys that yesterday he asked me to move in with him.

He's willing to take the boys on, and he's good to us; you should be pleased that somebody wants to take them off your hands. Don't worry; when I sell the house you'll get your half of the proceeds."

She could feel her face reddening with anger and with the effort of trying to speak. She opened the door to the sitting room and stood in the hallway.

"Marie and Freddie are probably wondering why you're not back yet."

"I'll go then."

He stood up slowly, looked around the room, and brushed past her on his way to the front door. She remembered when his nearness would make her tremble with desire, but now she felt only an irritation and a deep-seated antipathy. When she closed the door behind him she stood for a while, pressing her forehead against one of the cool glass panes. After a few moments she heard footsteps down the hallway.

"What was that all about?"   Alan came to stand beside her.

"Oh; a bit of the green-eyed monster I think. He left us a long time ago, but it appears he can't stand the thought of the three of us living with anybody else."

"Ha ha; he'd better get used to it." Alan kissed her and smiled.

"That's what I told him in so many words. We've got to tell the boys now before he phones and tells them himself."

"Okay; let's do it then."

They looked at each other and smiled as they made their way upstairs. Hand-in-hand, they walked along the landing and stood in the doorway of the boys' room.

"We've got some good news."

She watched the expression on her sons' faces as they looked up from their computer game.

"Are you getting married?" Kieran put down his joystick and waited expectantly.

"No, but Alan wants us to move in with him. He's got a bigger house and you boys will be able to have your own rooms. What do you say?"

"Great! I hate sleeping with Kev; he snores." Kieran nodded, punched his brother, and picked up his joystick.

"What do you say Kev?" Erin scrutinised her more sensitive son's face for any clues.

"I'm okay with it. Yes; it's fine."

She smiled as Kevin walked over towards them, shook Alan's hand, and gave her a cuddle.

"Good for you Mum; you deserve something nice happening to you for once."

At that point her eyes filled with tears, and she felt as if she could burst with happiness.

# CHAPTER 50

THE TREATMENT ROOM was too hot, and Erin felt trapped as she paced up and down. The thyrogen injections had worked their magic, there was no nausea, and she was full of boundless, unused energy. As she marched back and forth on the second day of incarceration, she looked around her room. Alan had stayed in this one; he had slept in her bed, and she could feel closer to him while sitting in his armchair and remembering how they had fitted the ballerina puzzle together. However, on this subsequent occasion everything was rather different; Alan was not in the room next door, and she had nobody to call on apart from a disabled and elderly man in his eighties who was stone deaf and depended on her to bring in his meals.

When the bell sounded at the hatch signalling breakfast, she went out into the lobby, picked up Albert's tray, and opened the door to his room. Pyjama-clad, he was seated in his armchair, staring straight ahead at nothing in particular. Erin placed the tray in front of him, smiled, and acknowledged his feeble wave before walking back out into the lobby and collecting her cereal, toast, and newspaper.

She put her tray down on her bedside table, and switched on the kettle. The hospital's free teabags had not been to her taste the first time around, and she was glad that Alan had reminded her to bring her favourite brand from home. While waiting for the water to boil she pulled her armchair over to the window, and stood on it in order to climb up onto the high, flat, window ledge.

Higher up now, she could see a few people in the offices opposite working at their computers. She noticed one of them watching her intently as she reached up and tried to open the small window above her head. To her delight the handle yielded under her fingers, and fresh, cool March air fell down upon her upturned face. Closing her eyes and imagining she was outside, she basked in the invigorating breeze. When climbing down onto the armchair again to make her tea she was amused to notice that several other people had been distracted by her antics who were supposed to be working.

Leaving the armchair where it was, she pulled her bedside table over to the window and enjoyed the change of air while she ate her breakfast. The toast was cold, but she reasoned that was the least of her worries. After reading the newspaper from cover to cover, even the hated sports pages, she looked up at the clock and saw that it was still only twenty minutes past ten. She sighed with boredom as she wondered who else was not busy and would enjoy a chat on the telephone; Alan and her various friends were working, the twins and Tilly were at college, and therefore all the rest of her morning would consist of would be either phoning her mother, washing up her cereal bowl and cup, or dying a little death and watching daytime TV.

Desperate for some human contact, she went out into the lobby and peeped around Albert's door. The old man had dressed himself in jogging bottoms and a jumper, and was now dozing in his armchair. She lifted his tray, took it over to the sink, and washed up his breakfast things. After leaving them draining by the sink she turned around to see him smiling at her.

"Hello Albert!" She whispered as loudly as she could.

She watched as Albert lifted up his right hand, palm facing her, and moved it around in a circular motion while mouthing *hello*. Without thinking she lifted up her right hand and did the same. The old man touched his chin with the fingers of his right hand, and then brought his arm downwards to the middle of his chest, palm facing upwards, while pointing with his other hand over towards the sink.

"What are you saying to me, Albert?"

Watching his lips as he performed the action again, Erin realised that Albert was thanking her. She went over to the sink and touched his clean cup and plate.

"You're thanking me for washing up your crockery?" She emphasised her lip movements.

The old man nodded, smiled, and lifted up the thumb of his right hand. Erin felt pleased that she had understood what he was trying to say. She then noticed that he was suddenly looking sad, and had made fists with both hands but had left the little fingers out, which were trailing down his chest as he yawned.

"You're tired?" Erin shrugged in case she had misunderstood.

The old man nodded, smiled, and once again lifted up the thumb of his right hand. Erin pointed to the kettle.

"Shall I make you a drink?"

She watched his mouth forming a word as the old man read her lips, nodded, and then made a 'c' shape with his right hand and brought it towards his face, tipping it backwards and forwards as he did so.

"You'd like some coffee?"

Albert smiled, nodded, and lifted up his right thumb, pleased at being able to communicate. After making some coffee and putting it beside him, she suddenly had an idea.

"Would you like to help me do a jigsaw puzzle?"

The old man looked blank. Emboldened, Erin lifted up the index finger of her right hand.

"Wait a minute."

She went out into the lobby and retrieved the now dismembered ballerina. Showing him the box, he made fists with both hands but left the thumbs out, which circled around each other at a distance.

"Ah…….that's the sign for puzzle!"

The old man smiled, nodded, and raised his right thumb.

She spent a pleasant morning rebuilding the ballerina with the old man, who eventually nodded off again in his armchair after lunch. After washing up their plates and leaving him with the half-completed jigsaw, she checked her phone on returning to her room.

*Will pop in for 20 minutes after lunch.'*

She cleaned her teeth and then sat back her window armchair, willing the door to open. When she eventually heard sounds out in the lobby, she lifted the blinds of her viewing window and peeped through before opening the door and grinning at Alan, who stood before her in a plastic overall, rubber gloves, and plastic overshoes.

"You look like a Yeti!"

"I'm sweating like a stuck pig already in this getup!"

"Come in then, and prepare to be irradiated."

"The nurse wouldn't let me in until I'd put all this clobber on."

"Be careful then, and stand near the door. I'll sit over by the window."

She quickly made her way to her armchair, and waved at him from across the room.

"I don't care about getting a dose, I just want to give you a kiss." Alan stood awkwardly, crinkling and rustling in his plastic suit.

"Bloody cheek! I haven't got a dose!" Erin feigned annoyance.

"Not that sort of dose you silly cow, the radiation dose."

"No, stay over there; I'm not safe. I don't want to be the one to give you leukaemia." Erin shook her head.

"I miss you so much." Alan sighed. "I want you home with me."

"You can pick me up tomorrow. I've got a puzzle to finish with my new boyfriend first."

Alan looked at her intently.

"Who's next door then?"

"He's lovely; he's called Albert."

"Albert eh? Have I got some competition then?"

"Yeah; he's in his eighties and stone deaf, but we've had a lovely morning." Erin smiled at him. "We're doing that blasted ballerina again."

"Ha!  She was a bitch, wasn't she?"  Alan chuckled.

"Yeah; I'm so looking forward to coming home though. How are the boys?" She drank in his facial features, ready to recall them as soon as he left.

"They cooked me some dinner last night. It was edible; not bad actually. I think it was chicken Kiev."

She laughed.

"They like you, don't worry; if they didn't they'd be round at Chris and Marie's all the time."

"They're okay. I've even found a way of telling them apart now."

"Oh?  How?"  She looked at him with interest.

"By their voices. Kieran is always more upbeat. Kevin is usually quieter and more serious."

"You've got it."

"Kevin was asking me this morning when you'd be home."

"I'll know more when the physicist has been at half past two, but I'm sure I'll be okay to go tomorrow."

"Good. I can't wait to feel your body on top of mine again. Oh, and Chris rang to speak to you last night. I think he'd forgotten you were in here."

"What does he want?" Erin felt a twinge of irritation at the mention of his name.

"He's asking how the sale of your house is going."

"I'll ring him; he's probably desperate for his share. I don't suppose we'll exchange contracts until next month at the earliest."

"I'll leave you to tell him that."

"Cheers."

A loud rapping on the outside door caused Erin to grimace.

"They want you to go now. Go on; bugger off before you fry."

"Can I ask one more thing before I go?" Alan put the fingers of his right hand around the door handle.

"Yeah, but make it quick. That Sister's a bit of a tartar."

He tore through the plastic overall, and with his left hand fished in the pocket of his jeans and brought out a small square box.

"Will you marry me? Last night apart from you was terrible. I love you so much, darling."

Open-mouthed, she looked towards him and then back at the box; finally feasting her eyes on the man she had come to adore over such a short space of time.

"Yes." She whispered while wiping sudden tears from her eyes and giving him a smile big enough to light up the sky. "You bet!"

# CHAPTER 51

ERIN NERVOUSLY TWISTED her new engagement ring around and around on the third finger of her left hand, as she sat next to Alan and faced the oncologist.

"Your new Gamma scan showed only uptake in the salivary glands and bladder; this, as you know, is normal. Your thyroglobulin levels have come right down, so at this moment in time Ms Mason, we can say that you are tentatively in remission. However, be aware that thyroid cancer can recur at any time, even five, ten or twenty years down the line. We will call you in for follow up appointments every three months for now, and then perhaps next year if all is well we will stretch it out to every six months."

She nodded with relief and felt Alan give her right hand a squeeze.

"Thank you, Doctor Ingram; so no more treatment at the moment then?"

"No; just keep taking your daily thyroxine tablet, and remember to have your bloods done before each follow up appointment."

She walked out of the consultation room as though she was floating on air.

"I'm so pleased for you darling; we need to have some sort of celebration now that we're both free of it." Alan smiled and put his arm around her as they walked back to the car park.

"We are; we're getting married don't forget!" Erin snuggled into his shoulder and pinched his behind.

"I mean now, not in August."

"Easter's coming up; how about we book a holiday away from hospitals, doctors, and treatment rooms?" He looked down at her and squeezed her shoulder.

"Maybe a short break; I don't want to take too much time off work."

"Okay; I understand."

"I've only been there a few months. I like the job."

"Sure; perhaps we'll rent a cottage on the coast for the Easter break? How about somewhere up in North Norfolk?" Alan looked at her and smiled.

"Why not? The boys are staying with Chris and Marie at Easter; we can go for a long weekend."

"Great; let's look online when we get back."

Kevin looked over their shoulders at the computer screen displaying places to visit in Norfolk.

"Are we going too?"

"Your mum and I are going when you stay with your dad at Easter." Alan answered matter-of-factly.

"Oh."

"I think Dad's booked a long weekend at Center Parcs for you all." Erin noticed the disappointment in Kevin's voice, and was eager to make amends.

"That's okay then!" Kevin smiled. "I'll see if I can beat Kieran down the rapids this time."

"What about Sheringham? We went there once when Tilly was into horses."

"No, I'd rather go somewhere that you haven't been with your ex, if that's okay with you?" Erin scrolled down. "What about Cromer? That's near to Sheringham. It looks like a nice seaside town."

"Right then; Cromer it is." Alan sniffed. "Have you been there with your ex?"

"Touché." Erin giggled. "No, but I fancied a chap once whose parents lived there."

"That's alright; it doesn't count."

# EPILOGUE

THE CRUEL EAST wind was biting as they stood on the beach facing the sea. Erin pulled a scarf a little more firmly around her neck, and turned her face towards Alan.

"This is better than being cooped up in the radioiodine room!" She tried to shout over the noise of the sea.

"Abso-blinking-lutely!" Alan wrapped his arms around her and looked down into her eyes.

"I love it here! This town is so quaint!"

"All I keep reading everywhere are notices about Cromer crabs. I hope I don't catch any." Alan chuckled and kissed the top of her head.

"Depends if you hang around on street corners." Erin opened the zip of his fleecy jacket and slid her arms around his chest.

"Let's walk along the Esplanade a bit, and then there's the pier and also a museum we could visit if you get too cold." Alan kept one arm around her shoulders as they walked.

"I can walk for miles; I just love being outside now." Erin took a deep breath of the salty air.

"Me too; there's something about being in that treatment room that does your head in, don't you think?"

"I don't think; I know. I was desperate to escape. It's probably because we couldn't go out that we both now have such a strong desire to be walking about in the fresh air." Erin nodded.

They carried on strolling in companionable silence for a while until they came to a sheltered bench.

"Let's sit here a minute." Alan sat down with a contented sigh.

"I'm having such a lovely day." Erin seated herself and looked out to sea.

"Me too." Alan took her hand in his and caressed her fingers.

Screeching seagulls flew overhead, circling them while looking for titbits.

"Do you ever worry about the cancer returning?" He kept his eyes on the choppy water.

"Sometimes, but then again it's probably best not to think about it. You could worry yourself into an early grave." Erin shrugged under her coat.

"You're right.   I just wonder sometimes if I've still got it."

"We're in remission now. We need to live our lives a day at a time and not think about the future." Erin linked her arm in his. "We're healthy at this point in time, and that's as good as it's going to get."

"I will love you for the rest of my life, however long that is." He kissed her lips.



A Rather Unusual Romance

"We'll have a long life together, don't you worry about that." She let her cheek touch his. "Not many people find their soul mate in this lifetime. I've found you, and right now the future's never looked better."

They stood up, linked arms again, and after a while any onlooker could not have distinguished them at all from the many other middle-aged couples walking along towards the pier.

## THE END

If you have enjoyed this story, you may also like 'A Marriage of Convenience' by Stevie Turner.

## REVIEW OF 'A MARRIAGE OF CONVENIENCE' BY STEVIE TURNER

"Turner has a gift for creating engrossing family drama stories and fleshing out strong characters who draw us into their stories and emotions.

In this tale we are introduced to Sophie, a university student, who is offered an unusual opportunity to marry Gerrie, an aspiring musician who is a fellow student at her school,: he's looking for someone who will marry him to give him legal status to stay in the U.K. legally to pursue his musical career. A large sum of money comes with the offer which makes it quite a tempting one.

What transpires from their marriage of convenience turns out to be a lasting love, along with an emotional rollercoaster for both Sophie and Gerrie from the beginning when they both, first have to inform their parents about the sudden marriage, and continues with the drama that ensues throughout their marriage (no spoilers). Suffice it to say, that the plot thickens when Gerrie hatches a plot to extract money from his wealthy parents to start up a band and take it on the road, which backfires because Gerrie's parents had bigger dreams of him taking over the family business, so there was no other way his parents would freely hand him over the money for a pipedream. This leaves Gerrie with no option but to go through with his alternate plan which ultimately winds up jeopardizing his family.

The story continues to build with many tribulations as the couple's plight to gain funds gets sticky, and Gerrie and Sophie are faced with dramatic family woes. As the years pass and their family grows, grief that is hidden but never forgotten plays a big part in their quest to regain their family unit and in doing so, find forgiveness for the baddies who had turned their lives upside down."
- *D.G Kaye*

# OTHER BOOKS BY STEVIE TURNER

THE PILATES CLASS

A HOUSE WITHOUT WINDOWS

FOR THE SAKE OF A CHILD

LILY: A SHORT STORY

NO SEX PLEASE, I'M MENOPAUSAL!

A MARRIAGE OF CONVENIENCE

THE DAUGHTER-IN-LAW SYNDROME

REVENGE

THE NOISE EFFECT: A SHORT STORY

THE DONOR

LIFE: 18 SHORT STORIES

WAITING IN THE WINGS

MIND GAMES

REPENT AT LEISURE

A NOVELLA COLLECTION

CRUISING DANGER

ALYS IN HUNGER-LAND